A Tidbit of Trust

Taste of Romance Book 5

Elizabeth Maddrey

2017

Scripture quoted by permission. Quotations designated (NIV) are from THE HOLY BIBLE: NEW INTERNATIONAL VERSION®. NIV®. Copyright © 1973, 1978, 1984 by Biblica. All rights reserved worldwide.

Cover design ©Elizabeth Maddrey.
Cover art photos via DepositPhotos.com ©ankamonika, ©mimagephotos, ©sumners used by permission.

Published in the United States of America by Elizabeth Maddrey
www.ElizabethMaddrey.com

Other Books by Elizabeth Maddrey

Arcadia Valley Romance – Baxter Family Bakery Series
Loaves & Wishes (in Romance Grows in Arcadia Valley)
Muffins & Moonbeams
Cookies & Candlelight
Donuts & Daydreams (March 2018)

The 'Operation Romance' Series
Operation Mistletoe
Operation Valentine
Operation Fireworks
Operation Back-to-School

The 'Taste of Romance' Series
A Splash of Substance
A Pinch of Promise
A Dash of Daring
A Handful of Hope
A Tidbit of Trust

The 'Grant Us Grace' Series
Joint Venture
Wisdom to Know
Courage to Change
Serenity to Accept

The 'Remnants' Series:
Faith Departed
Hope Deferred
Love Defined

Stand alone novellas
Kinsale Kisses: An Irish Romance

Non-Fiction
A Walk in the Valley: Christian encouragement for your journey
through infertility

For the most recent listing of all my books, please visit my website.

For everyone who has ever struggled to understand God's grace.

It is there. It is real. He loves you.

1

Sara Reynolds slipped on her sunglasses and stepped out of her hotel room onto the beach. This was the perfect way to spend the week between Christmas and New Year's. Sun, sand, and absolutely no plans. Of course, it would be better with friends—which had been the original plan before Rebecca and Jen met guys, fell in love, and ruined everything. Sara blew out a breath. Maybe that wasn't fair, but it wasn't exactly fair that she was alone in Jamaica on what was supposed to have been their girls' trip. Okay, sure, they'd never put an actual date on the excursion, but they'd discussed it enough over the years that when she'd mentioned the idea in September she'd expected a little more enthusiasm. Obviously, as pregnant as she'd been, Rebecca had been out. She'd finally given birth to her little girl, Chloe, just last week. But Jen was getting married on Valentine's Day, which meant she ought to have been ready for one final fling. Right?

She walked across the warm sand to a row of lounge chairs and dragged one a little bit away from the rest. The beach wasn't busy yet, but everything she'd read online prior to booking said the resort was always at capacity this week and she didn't intend to be smashed up against other sunbathers like sardines in a can.

Her therapist, at least, was proud of her for coming alone. Sara had been single since the debacle with Luc last spring. Her stomach twisted as his face swam unbidden into her thoughts. He was supposed to have been *the one*. Not the one who strung her along as his stateside girlfriend while he kept a wife at home and who knew how many other women across the globe. He travelled for a living—well, he had. At least he'd been fired after his behavior was made public. Regardless, Dr. Thomason said Sara's willingness to travel by herself was indicative of progress.

"Miss? Can I get you anything?" The lilting Jamaican accent from the roving server made her smile.

"No, thank you."

"Are you going to Dunn's River Falls today? They still have seats on the shuttle. If you want to go, I can book you."

Sara stared out at the ocean. The waterfall was famous. Everything online said visitors couldn't come to Jamaica and *not* go. But...it was her first day here. "They're going again later in the week, right?"

The young man pursed his lips. "I'm not sure. Would you like me to get you a schedule?"

"Sure. Thanks."

He grinned, his white teeth gleaming in stark contrast to his dark skin. "I'll be right back."

She adjusted the lounge chair so it reclined more and closed her eyes. Even as handsome as the man had been, she'd had no desire to flirt. That had to be progress, too. She wasn't here to hook up. Maybe that would've been a serious consideration a year ago but...she was changing. Trying to at least.

"Here, miss."

Sara opened her eyes and took the schedule with a smile. She skimmed the various tour options and sighed. There wasn't another trip to the falls through the resort until her last day. And the timing of that would make it a challenge to be at the airport with enough lead time. She could always get a taxi and go on her own, but..."You said there's still room to go today?"

He nodded.

"Then if you'd sign me up, I'd appreciate it. I'm in 461."

"Yes, miss. Meet in the front lobby at ten-thirty. Do you want a sack lunch?"

"Is there food there?"

He nodded. "There are local vendors. For sure some will have patties, maybe there will be someone grilling."

"I'll give the locals a try." She was here, after all, for adventure. And if it didn't sit well, she could stay on the resort for the rest of her stay with a free conscience. "Thanks."

He bobbed his head again and drifted off toward a couple who was busily setting up a home away from home on the sand. Sara stood and collected her towel. If she was catching a shuttle at ten-thirty, she'd best go change.

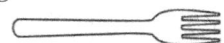

The resort wasn't far from the falls. It had taken maybe twenty minutes to get to the parking area. Now she stood in the crowd with all the others who had been on the shuttle listening to last minute instructions.

"As we climb the falls, you need to hold hands with the person in front of you and the person behind you. We'll climb like that in a chain. If you start to slip, the people on either side should be able to help. But most of all don't panic." The guide grinned. "This is supposed to be fun."

Sara frowned. She hadn't realized they'd have to go up as a group. That's what she got for not reading the excursion information more carefully. Ah well, it was a once-in-a-lifetime experience, right? At least there wasn't a cruise ship in port today, flooding the area with even more people working their way up the rocks as water crashed over them. In fact, Sara only saw one other group lining up. Even if her group was second in line, the whole trek shouldn't take more than an hour. That left plenty of time to poke through the long line of stalls manned by local craftspeople and to find something to eat. Then she could honestly tell everyone that she hadn't stayed in the resort her entire vacation. Win-win.

Sara moved into the line as it formed and took the hand of the man in front of her. His wife, maybe girlfriend, was in front of him and fixed Sara with a frown. What was she supposed to do? The guides were walking down the line making sure everyone was holding hands. Maybe going on excursions like this wasn't a great idea for couples who didn't like other people.

The woman behind her tapped her shoulder and offered her hand with a smile. At least some people were friendly.

The group ahead of them, composed mostly of teenagers from what Sara could see, was finally on its way up the falls, which meant their group could now begin the trek. The water was cold. Colder than she'd expected. She certainly wasn't going to be getting any wetter than she had to on this climb. She'd save any water sports for the ocean. She could snorkel just off the beach outside her room without freezing to death.

Up ahead, a girl shrieked and slipped off a rock into a pool between levels of the falls. Sara winced and looked down at her footing, watching where she put her feet more carefully. Of course, that kept her from doing much looking around. This was supposed to be a beautiful climb and she was missing most of it.

When they reached the mid-point, the guide gestured for them to drop hands. "We'll take a short rest here. You can sit, if you want to."

Sara shook her head and turned to look up the remainder of the falls. The group ahead of them was nearing the top. The rush of water over the rocks was breathtaking. God sure made amazing things. She turned and looked down over what they'd already climbed, her eyes widening at the height.

"All right, form back up and let's continue," the guide hollered from the front of the group.

Some groaned as they stood. The man in front of her didn't reach back for her hand. That was fine. Sara was managing okay without his help, and she didn't particularly want to deal with the death glares his wife had shot her way for the first half of the trek.

There were a few more slips and splashes—not all accidental, as the guides were urging people to jump in at various spots—before they reached the top. Sara turned and looked back down, following the falls as they splashed against the rocks and threw rainbows into the air, then let her gaze drift across the beach to the ocean.

"I can't...it hurts." The words, punctuated by sobs, made Sara turn. A teenage girl leaned against a large rock, with one foot off the ground. A man about Sara's age with a grim look on his face stood beside her.

"It's not far to the van. We'll head back to the church and...maybe they can call a doctor. I'll have to check with the pastor and see what he recommends."

Sara crossed to them, wiping her hands on her damp shorts. "Hi. I overheard a little. Maybe I can help?"

"Are you a doctor?" The man's eyebrows lifted, hope evident in his expression.

"No. But I'm a physical therapist. I can probably tell you if something's broken. What hurts?"

The girl sniffled. "My ankle. It got caught between some rocks as I climbed."

Sara squatted and lifted the girl's foot. The fact that she could put it down, even with very little pressure on it, was a good sign. It wasn't very swollen and though it caused a few whimpers, it had full range of motion with no popping or grinding sounds. Sara stood and faced the man. "I think it's a sprain, worst case. If your daughter stays off it for the rest of today she should be fine tomorrow. If you can find an elastic wrap and elevate it with ice, that'll be even better."

"She's not my daughter. But we can manage the bandage and ice." He turned to look at the girl. "You're going to be okay. Maybe you can help with the puppet show for the kids tonight instead of the soccer game we were going to organize."

"Okay, Adam." The girl wiped a tear off her cheek and tried to stand, peering up at Adam through her lashes. "I think I'm going to need help getting to the van though."

Adam cleared his throat, pink heating his cheeks. "Maybe I can find Molly and she can carry you on her back."

Sara stifled a smile. Apparently Adam had caught the subtle flirtation and was backing away as fast as he could. "What if she leaned on me? I can help, we'll follow you, and that'll get her to a place to put her foot up faster than if you have to go find someone else and bring them back here."

He studied Sara before nodding. "Okay. Thanks..."

"Sara. Sara Reynolds." She stuck out her hand.

"Adam Lassiter." A shiver raced through her as he took her hand firmly in his. Must be a delayed reaction to the cold water of the falls. The sooner she got this girl to their van and herself on the shuttle back to her resort, the better. She obviously needed dry clothes and time in the sun.

2

Adam wove through the crowds of tourists and local artisans who were hawking their wares—some more aggressively than others. He rubbed his still-tingling palm on his pants and frowned. Sara Reynolds. What were the odds?

Of course, she wasn't down here helping the youth group on their winter break mission trip. Oh, no. She was probably set up in one of the swanky resorts that dotted the island, completely oblivious to the poverty outside the walls. That was exactly how he wanted it, of course.

She hadn't recognized him.

That stung. Not that he'd had anything but scorn for the jolt of recognition that had worked its way through him when he'd spotted her at the falls. But they'd been attending the same singles class for going on three years now. Was it too much to expect her to at least think he looked familiar?

Adam glanced over his shoulder.

Sara grinned and waved off another vendor as she and Melody hobbled down the path to the exit.

Who had approved Melody's application for this trip? He hadn't, that was certain. And he wouldn't have if it had gone through the full screening like all the others did. Adam spent enough time working with the youth to know the only reason the girl had even wanted to come was to flirt with the boys. Or the male leaders. She was obviously lacking male attention at home, and that broke his heart, but it made being her youth leader tricky. He tried to be positive and encouraging, to let her see that there were men who could and did value her as a daughter of God. But she took any attention and tried to twist it into flirtation. In that respect, she was a miniature version of Sara Reynolds in the making. Although—he cast a quick look behind him as if there was a way for Sara to overhear his thoughts—rumor had it that she'd settled down some since the spring. Not that he cared. At all.

He sighed when he finally spotted the church van. Molly was perched on the floor, her feet dangling out the open side door. At least he wouldn't have to stay with Melody and risk another of her attempts to bat her eyelashes at him. He'd drop the girl here and then head back in to round up the rest of the crew. They'd taken the morning off to sightsee since this was the only day this week without cruise ships scheduled, but the church expected them back for afternoon and evening activities.

"Hey. Where's everyone else?" Molly frowned. "Is that Sara Reynolds?"

Adam nodded. "Melody hurt her ankle. Sara showed up and offered to help, which was a blessing since Melody isn't in enough pain to stop her from batting her eyelashes."

Molly snickered. "You're male and breathing, those are her two major criteria."

"Tell me." Adam stepped back as Sara and Melody finally made it to the car.

"Here you go." Sara slipped her arm out from under the girl's and stepped back. "I really think if you keep it wrapped, iced, and elevated tonight you'll be as good as new tomorrow."

"We can do that. Sara, right?" Molly hopped out of the van and gave Melody a boost up. "Good to see you."

Adam smothered a chuckle and turned to watch Sara's reaction. Her face was blank. Typical.

"Yeah, okay." Sara turned to Adam and managed a small smile. "Don't forget the ice."

"Got it. Thanks, by the way." Adam tucked his hands in the pockets of his cargo shorts. This was awkward. Should he tell her they knew each other? Well, they obviously *didn't*...but they should or could or...yeah. Better to just leave it alone.

Molly punched his arm as Sara ambled toward the resort shuttle parking. Sure enough, she knocked on the door to one of the best and climbed in. "That's it? Thanks by the way?"

"What else is there to say?" Adam shrugged. "I'm going to go round everyone else up."

Shaking her head, Molly hopped back into the van. "Yeah, you do that."

"What's up with you? You've been extra quiet all night." Molly lowered herself to the ground beside Adam and leaned against the outside wall of the church, mimicking his pose.

"Just thinking." Adam smiled as a breeze kicked through the leaves of the palm trees, stirring the air and cooling it some. It was weird to be hot in December, but the temperatures had been in the mid-80s since they had landed two days ago, and it was likely they'd continue the rest of the trip.

"About a certain woman from church, I imagine."

Why couldn't he fall in love with Molly? He'd tried. They'd even gone out a handful of times, but at the end, they'd had to admit they'd never be more than friends. He'd been content to keep dating—maybe even get married eventually—with things the way they were between them, but Molly said she was holding out for explosive passion. It sounded painful. And he was pretty sure he didn't have that in him. "I thought you told me there was no chemistry and I should quit pining for you."

"Ha ha. You know who I mean."

He shrugged. "It was just weird seeing her here. How did Mel's ankle look when you got the girls settled and lights out?"

"Changing the subject. Interesting. As it happens, there's very little swelling and half the time she forgets which leg she's supposed to be limping on, so I don't think it's even sprained. Just twisted." Molly drummed her fingers on her knee. "For what it's worth, I like Sara's friends. I don't know them super well, but Jen has made a few overtures and seems nice."

Which meant exactly nothing. "You can have friends and still be a horrible person."

"She's a horrible person? I don't get that at all."

Yeah, well, guys talked. More than girls did, apparently. Adam had heard the rumors. Sara's name and number might as well have been scribbled in the bathroom under the words "for a good time call." That was absolutely not the kind of woman he was looking for. "Horrible might be overstated. She's just not my type."

"Mmmm." Molly nodded.

Adam waited, but she didn't continue. Crickets started up a discordant symphony. "All right, I'll bite. What's that mean?"

"I think...you should give her a break. People can change."

Maybe girls did talk, after all. "Of course they can."

Molly opened her mouth but was interrupted by a chirping of Adam's watch.

He stood and offered a hand to help her up. "Time for evening devotions with the pastor and the rest of the chaperones."

"Think about what I said." Molly took his hand and tugged herself up. "*Pray* about it."

He could do that. Since every day he felt a stronger, heavier call to some kind of ministry, he was pretty certain there was no way God wanted him getting involved with Sara Reynolds.

Adam joined the circle of leaders in the main room of the church and tried to picture Sara as a missionary. Or a pastor's wife. It was like imagining a lizard as a rodeo clown. His efforts dissolved into an image of Sara in the moonlight wrapped in his arms. He pushed it away and bowed his head, forcing his attention away from the easily recalled sensation of her hand in his to the Jamaican pastor's prayer.

A physical temptation was *not* going to distract him from God's call.

3

Sara wandered down the length of the buffet with her empty tray. Nothing was interesting. She'd had a decent lunch and spent the bulk of her day either lying in the sun or snorkeling in the ocean. Maybe she simply hadn't done enough to need to eat again. Blowing out a breath, she carried the tray back to the start of the line and dropped it on the pile before she exited the dining area. Now what?

She strolled across the sand toward her room. If she was at home she'd just be leaving work and Rebecca would be cajoling her into going to the Wednesday night service at church with her and Ben. Everyone would be there—except maybe Paige. Her restaurant, Season's Bounty, did a surprising amount of business on Wednesday nights, so she had to be there. Well, and Zach and Amy. They'd found a church in D.C., near where they lived, and attended there now. They probably went every time the doors were open, though. So really it was just Jackson, Rebecca and Ben, and Jen and David. But that was usually enough to entice her to go. Then they'd all get dinner together afterward. Maybe...

Before she could change her mind, Sara shifted direction and headed for the front desk. There was no one there. She tapped the small, silver bell on the counter and waited.

"Hello. Sorry." An older woman scurried from the open door that must lead to the office. "How can I help you?"

"I was wondering—and I realize this might be odd—do any of the nearby churches have a Wednesday night service that a tourist would be welcome at?" Sara brushed at her shorts. Had she even brought something that would be appropriate for church? This outfit would be fine at home, but maybe churches here were more formal?

The woman beamed and opened a fat binder. She flipped several pages before removing a typed page. "Of course. Here's a list with times and the address. They're grouped by denomination. If you want to order a taxi, just let us know and we'll take care of it."

"Do you—is it dressy?" Sara took the list and fought against the weight building up in her chest.

"The ones that are have it marked by them. See here?" The woman leaned across the counter and tapped an entry with a double asterisk by it.

She'd just avoid those. "Thanks."

Sara carried the list to one of the groupings of white wicker chairs that graced the marble lobby and sat. There weren't actually that many churches that indicated a need for more formal attire. That was good. Except that it made narrowing her choices a little trickier. She scanned the denominations and frowned. Her church at home was non-denominational, although there were roots in one of the bigger ones. So maybe that was the place to start? Or maybe this was just a bad idea.

She tugged her cell phone out of her pocket and stared at it. She could text Rebecca. It would cost a mint, but maybe it'd be worth it. Maybe her friend would actually check the built-in messaging app for the social media site they were all part of; then, at least, it'd be free. She tapped the familiar blue icon and ignored the red square that screamed an amazing number of notifications since she last checked in. Well, she still wasn't checking. She was on vacation. She just needed advice.

With a silent plea—did it count as a prayer?—for Rebecca to be online, Sara tapped a quick message.

"Thinking of going to church down here tonight—can't decide where. Thoughts?"

The little dancing ellipsis that meant Rebecca was typing back came up almost immediately. After a moment, her reply was there, "Do it."

Okay. Great. "But where? Have a list from the resort, but no clue how to choose."

"Is Fellowship of Grace on there?"

Why did Rebecca know the name of a church in Jamaica? Sara scanned the list. It was there, the only listing in the non-denominational section. She typed back, "Yeah?"

"Go there. They're our sister church."

Sister church? What...? It didn't matter. It was a recommendation and that's what she'd been looking for. And looking at the sheet, she didn't have a lot of time to ponder if she wasn't going to be slinking in the back late. "Thanks."

"Anytime. When you get a minute, let us know how your vacation is going. Had lunch with a couple of girls from work, they said Mr. Phillips, in particular, misses you."

Sara snorted and turned off her phone. Mr. Phillips was the only one of her physical therapy clients she was guaranteed not to miss, not with his tendency to look for any opportunity to pinch her behind.

The taxi was there almost as soon as the woman at the desk was finished calling them and it was a relatively short drive to the church. Sara spent the time looking out the window. It was amazing the difference between the resort areas and the places where the locals lived. The houses nearest the resort were walled in with bars and windows on the doors. When they'd left the near area, there was a stark transition to...poverty. There was no other word to use. And yet the people on the street went about their business because this was, clearly, all they knew.

"Here you are. I be back in two hours to take you to the hotel. Don't go walkin' in this part of town, now." The taxi driver waved off her payment. "It's billed to your room. We have a special deal."

"Okay. Thanks." Sara took a deep breath as she exited the cab and stared at the building. It wasn't anything like she expected—just a plain, gray, concrete structure with a small sign above the door.

Inside wasn't much different. The walls were more of the concrete, unpainted and, largely, undecorated. Maybe this was a bad idea. She turned. The taxi was gone. Of course. Fine. She'd slip in the back and try to remain unobserved.

"Sara?" The woman from the van yesterday grinned as she crossed the...well, it was probably called the foyer, even if it didn't match up to what Sara was used to. "I'm Molly?"

"Right. Hi. How's the girl? I never did catch her name." Would they think that was why she'd shown up? Not that there was any way for her to have known this was where to come. Her stomach tightened, and a fleet of frogs started jumping up and down inside it.

Molly snickered. "Melody. And she's fine, much to her disappointment. She only managed to get one evening of special treatment out of it. And that sounds horrible. I'm sorry. She just wears on my patience. Which is also horrible."

The corners of Sara's mouth lifted. "It's okay. I have trouble thinking before I speak, too."

Molly laughed. "I see that. You don't remember me at all, do you?"

From yesterday? She'd brought up where they met...wasn't that enough to show she remembered? "I'm not following."

"We go to the same church in the States. Same Sunday school class, for that matter. Definitely not the same circles though."

Heat crawled up Sara's neck and spread across her cheeks. "Oh. I'm sorry. I...tend to stick in the same little group."

"So do I. It's no biggie. But Adam was a little put out that you didn't recognize him."

Adam? The hot guy who'd been haunting her thoughts since her time at the falls. "He doesn't..."

Molly nodded. "He does. The youth group is on a week-long mission trip over Christmas break. They asked in class for volunteers to chaperone."

That was...vaguely familiar. She hadn't paid a ton of attention since she already had this trip planned. And with most of her friends pairing off, getting married, and moving to couples classes, the singles group held a lot less appeal these days. She skipped almost as often as she attended. She wasn't looking for the same thing she had been and at this point, her reputation in there was basically wrecked. "Ah. I was just going to sit in the back until my taxi came back for me. Don't let me keep you."

"Don't be ridiculous. Come sit with the rest of the group. You can check on Melody's ankle and..."

"I'd really rather not. I'm embarrassed enough that I didn't recognize you. Look, I'll just call the resort and get them to send my taxi back. This was a bad idea. Um. I hope your trip is productive." Sara turned and fled out the front door, reaching in her purse for her phone. Why did the earth never open up and swallow her when she needed it most? And of course there was no wi-fi out here, which meant she couldn't pull up their website to get their phone number.

She could walk back. Except the driver had told her not to wander around and, well, the reality was it didn't exactly look safe. Which left her with two options. She could face the mortification sure to arise and go back in, sit in the back, and try to at least accomplish what she'd set out to do in the first place. Or she could stand out here until the taxi came back. Sara glanced around the darkening, deserted streets. A clump of kids came running from down the block, laughing and calling out insults to one another. They were probably harmless, but...no.

Door number two it was.

Sara glanced around. No benches, of course. She moved toward the corner of the building and leaned against the wall.

The door opened. Sara tried to shrink into the shadows. Would Molly follow her out here? Surely the woman had other things she needed to be doing.

But it wasn't Molly. A Jamaican woman limped through the door with a gusty sigh. She leaned over and massaged her knee before taking a few halting steps in a circle.

Sara couldn't stop herself from speaking. "Are you all right?"

The woman jolted and stepped toward Sara. "Fine, yes. My knee acts up in the air conditioning. They were so proud to install that—completely paid for by a church in the U.S., you know? And I'll admit it's nice in the summer, except it makes my knee ache."

"Have you injured it?" There were a lot of things that could make a joint cold sensitive, age being one of them. But as she moved closer, Sara discounted that. The woman was middle-aged, at best. Too young to have an aching knee unless there was an underlying medical condition.

She chuckled. "More times than I can count. I scrub houses in the city and am down on my knees all day."

"I might have some exercises that could help. At least a little. Can I show you?" Sara mentally ran through the options that seemed most likely, discarding anything that needed extra equipment. There were still a handful that might help. They certainly wouldn't hurt.

"Sure. It's always nice to try new things."

Sara laughed. "You might not say that after you've tried them for a week. We need a chair."

"One minute." The woman hobbled inside and was back out before much time had passed with a folding chair. "There are always empty seats in the back row."

"Okay." Sara opened the chair and gestured for the woman to sit. "This is the first one."

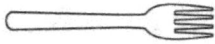

"Miss Sara?"

Sara opened her eyes and smiled at the beach attendant. He'd been very kind so far throughout her stay—she needed to remember to tip him when she checked out. "Yes?"

"You have a visitor in the main lobby."

Who could possibly be visiting her? She didn't know anyone here. Well, that wasn't completely true, but why would Molly or Adam come here? How would they even know where she was staying? She'd told the woman she helped last night, in case she'd had questions and needed to call. But she wouldn't stop by, would she? "I don't...did they give a name?"

"No Miss. I can ask, if you like."

She shook her head. He had other guests to see to, and some of them were incredibly demanding. "It's okay, I'll go see. Thank you for letting me know."

Sara stood and slipped a maxi dress over her bathing suit and headed toward the lobby. Her mother would be proud of her for having on a one-piece bathing suit. She got odd looks from many of the other resort guests, but the looks—and in some cases propositions—she'd gotten the first day when she'd returned from climbing the falls had convinced her that she was better off. It had changed her attitude some, as well, if she was honest. She certainly hadn't been spending as much time watching people to see if they were watching her and wondering if they liked what they saw. Maybe there was something to modesty after all.

She was angling toward the front desk when her gaze landed on him. Her belly quivered. How was it possible that she'd never noticed him at church? Tall, with a mop of curly chestnut hair and movie-star quality five o'clock shadow that made his blue eyes stand out, Adam was a sight that was hard to resist. But why was he here?

"Hi, Adam. Everything okay?" Sara fought to squash a cringe. What a lame opening.

He turned and his eyes widened ever so slightly, but he didn't smile. "What do you think you're doing?"

"Taking a vacation. What's it to you?" She crossed her arms and frowned. He might be good looking, but he could sure use help in the personality department.

He scowled. "That wasn't what I meant and you know it."

"No. I don't. Why are you here, Adam?"

"I'm here with a group of teens to help a local church. I'm talking to you to figure out why the pastor of that church is suddenly asking if our physical therapist can schedule a time to meet with people and suggest some exercises for them to do." He threw his hands in the air. "We have enough on our plate with the previously agreed on activities. I don't have time to babysit some vacationing glory hound!"

"I see." Sara clenched her teeth together and drew a breath in through her nose. She wasn't going to give him the satisfaction of seeing that he'd gotten to her, even if her blood was boiling. "Thank you for bringing it to my attention. I'll give the pastor a call and make arrangements. No babysitting necessary. Have a nice day."

"Don't you walk away." Adam reached out and grabbed her arm as Sara started to escape back to the beach.

She hissed through her teeth. "Get your hands off me."

Adam dropped his hand, his face pale. "Look. You can't just swoop in and offer unsolicited medical advice like this. You're not even a doctor. I realize you don't care if you hurt someone, but I do. These people are special. The work we're doing here is important."

Sara swallowed and raised a hand, cutting off his tirade. "I get the point. Goodbye, Adam."

She stalked quickly across the lobby, ignoring his repeated shouts of her name. Back on the beach, in the area of the resort where he couldn't follow, Sara sank to a lounge chair and buried her head in her hands. She'd just been trying to help.

No. She *had* helped.

And she could help others, too. She'd only said the bit about calling the pastor to get a dig in, but maybe it was worth doing. Sure, she wasn't a medical doctor, but she'd made that clear, both when she helped the teen and when she'd talked to the older lady at the church. Back home, medical doctors sent people to work with her on purpose. She knew what she was doing, and darn it, she *did* care if she hurt people. She also cared when people were hurting.

He didn't know her—didn't know anything about her...so why did Adam's words make her heart ache?

4

Adam stormed through the doors to the church, scooped up his tool belt, and stalked toward the sounds of industry behind the building. He paused and surveyed the team. Most of the kids had gone with Molly and the other leaders to a village about thirty minutes away to do evangelism and a day camp for kids. Only a handful of the guys had stayed behind to finish the four new Sunday school classrooms, such as they were.

Each building was an eight by sixteen foot rectangle made, essentially, of two by fours and plywood. The pastor insisted they were more than adequate, and, in fact, would rival some of the homes that people in the congregation lived in. Adam had yet to wrap his mind around it. They were cutting holes for windows, but no glass was planned. They'd provide ventilation, true, and also rain, humidity, and bugs. But Adam hadn't been able to convince anyone to veer from the original plans.

Taking a deep breath, Adam strapped on the belt and pushed Sara from his mind. Sure, she'd looked like a cool breath of air in that dress that floated around her ankles covering up who knew what kind of swim suit. Probably some tiny little bikini. The image that flashed through his brain left his mouth dry. He shook his head. It didn't matter that she was gorgeous, she was the church slut. Everyone knew Sara was the woman to call if you wanted to hook up. Sure, you had to pretend to have a relationship for a little while, but the scuttlebutt said two or three weeks was usually enough. That wasn't the kind of woman he wanted in his life.

"Are you going to stand there and daydream or help with the walls?" Pastor Lonzo grinned down from his perch on top of one of the new buildings.

Adam started. "Help, of course. Where do you need me?"

Lonzo pointed to the far building where three teenage boys struggled to heft a sheet of plywood into place. "They are having the most trouble, it seems. Did you accomplish your mission?"

His mission. Sara. He swallowed and shook his head. "I don't think she's going to give up her vacation time. I'm sorry."

The pastor frowned. "Ah well. It was worth a shot. Perhaps the next time I speak with your mission team coordinator I'll suggest adding on a medical component. We don't have many needs, but there are probably enough to justify a special trip."

"I'll try to remember to include that in my report." Adam slipped his hammer from the loop on his tool belt and headed over to help the boys.

Adam tried not to snort. Like Sara would ever go on a medical mission trip. First, she wasn't a medical practitioner. She was just a physical therapist. Did she even have to go to school for that, or was it a certificate she picked up from an eight-week class? Second, she wasn't exactly the giving type, not unless it benefitted her. And third? He shook his head, there was probably a third, fourth, and maybe even fifth reason she was a bad choice for something like that. He just happened to have more to do with his time than sit and figure out what they were.

By dinner, Adam was exhausted and drenched with sweat. The humidity in the air clung to him, making it hard to cool off. He wanted a shower and a quiet evening, preferably alone. What he had waiting for him was a scrub with water out of a rain barrel and team-building games followed by group devotions. At least once the kids were in bed he could steal a few minutes to himself. If he could avoid Molly.

"How'd your errand go this morning?" Molly jabbed him in the ribs with her elbow.

He grunted. So much for avoiding her. "I need to go wash. It's the guys' turn right now."

She lifted a brow. "That good? Can't wait to hear the whole story at dinner."

Right. He'd have to figure out some way to get past that. Adam ducked into the room the boys were sharing and dug through his duffel for a dry washcloth. At least the water in the rain barrels wasn't freezing. It wouldn't cool him off, but it would get rid of the sweat. If he worked a little, he could pretend he was clean. First thing he was doing when he got home was taking a long, hot shower.

The guys weren't big on the bucket wash, so the barrels were deserted when he arrived. Adam shook his head. Teenage boys had strange ideas about hygiene and its impact on one's ability to get close to the opposite sex. Not that he or any of the other chaperones wanted romance to bloom on the trip. They continued to have problems with one or two couples who tried to sneak off, but they'd been warned ahead of time that that was to be expected. So it was just a matter of keeping eyes open. And pulling his sleeping bag in front of the door when he went to bed.

After changing into the outfit he kept for evenings, Adam wandered out to the multi-purpose room that doubled as the sanctuary. Long, collapsible tables stretched down one side of the room, and local ladies were in the process of piling them with serving dishes heaped with food. The menu wasn't varied, but it was ample. Rice and peas—mixed together—factored heavily each night, as did some sort of spicy fish. One evening they'd had patties. He'd enjoyed those hand-held meat pies until he'd overheard the ladies say the filling was goat.

"There you are." Molly pulled him into a corner. "The kids are all helping bring in the VBS supplies from the van. They need to put the rest of the seats back in so they can use it for something else tonight. Tell me about your visit to Sara."

"There's nothing to tell. I went, we talked, she isn't doing it." Adam crossed his arms. Why did Molly care so much?

She frowned. "Really? I thought for sure she'd be up for it. Maybe I should've been the one to go ask."

"Absolutely not." He huffed out a breath. "Look, we have enough on our plate, don't you think? It's Thursday night and we're leaving bright and early Saturday morning. That gives us exactly tomorrow. When were we supposed to cram something else in? You're leading more street ministry, there's a group heading out for beach sports evangelism, and the classrooms are almost finished, but they'll take the rest of the day to get done."

"But what about *her* schedule? It's not as if we have to be here. Just imagine if she could help some of these people with simple exercises they can do on their own. Maybe it wouldn't be a perfect fix, but it'd be better than nothing." Molly's shoulders slumped. "I was really hoping the changes I'd seen and heard about her were real."

Adam shook his head. "People don't change, Molly. Not that dramatically."

"You really believe that?"

"Don't you?"

"No. Because if people can't change, then there's no point to Jesus." Molly turned on her heel and strode toward the group of girls loaded down with boxes of supplies.

Adam pursed his lips. Of course he believed Jesus could change people when they came to Him as a new believer. But when people said they believed and sinned anyway? Didn't that make it pretty obvious they weren't going to let Jesus work in their lives?

He shook his head. It didn't matter. He'd made it clear that Sara shouldn't come near this project. She was better off staying in her ritzy resort working on a tan. They were all better off.

Adam dumped the contents of his suitcase into the washing machine and spun the dial. He could practically hear his mother reminding him to sort by color and use different temperatures for different fabric types, but one big load on cold had served him well enough since college. Why mess with a good thing?

He shoved the empty bag into his closet and made his way into the bathroom attached to his bedroom. He'd won the coin toss for this bedroom when they first moved in, and even the exhaustion from a full last day in Jamaica and the inevitable chaos of herding teenagers through two airports and making sure they were all picked up by the right people couldn't wipe away the smile that came with the memory. Karl never seemed to share his joy. Some people were just sore losers.

The hot water pounded on his head. Heaven. After a week of sloshing around in a rain barrel—he shuddered and tried one more time to erase the dark thoughts of what parasites might have been sharing that water with him—this was heaven.

The toilet flushed.

"Hey!" Adam stepped out of the scalding spray and peeked out from behind the curtain. "What the heck, Karl?"

"Just wanted to say welcome home, man. You hungry?"

"As long as it's not fish or goat, yeah."

Karl grinned. "I got a bucket of chicken with all the sides. Hurry up and get dressed."

Adam reached for his shampoo and worked up a thick lather. He really needed to remember to lock his door when he was showering. Karl was a serious prankster. And that reminded him to check his bed carefully before he got in it tonight. The last time Adam had gone away for more than one night, he'd come home to find his bed short-sheeted.

He hurried through the rest of his shower and dressed in sweats and a college sweatshirt. The chilly D.C. weather was a shock after the humid, summer-like days in Jamaica.

The smell of fried chicken hit his nose as soon as he opened the door to his bedroom. Was there anything better than that? He grabbed a plate out of the kitchen cabinet and sat at the rickety table they'd found on the curb. It wasn't glamorous, but it did the trick. "This is great. I'm glad you thought of it."

Karl peered in the bucket and snagged three drumsticks. "Me too. I was driving by and it sort of called to me. Figured if you weren't home yet it tastes just as good cold."

"Maybe better. I never can decide." Adam bit into the chicken thigh and closed his eyes. Oh, yeah. He wiped a drip of juice off his chin and reached for the smaller containers. He pushed the green beans back across the table before scooping mac and cheese onto his plate. "Why do you get the beans? I don't eat them and you complain about having to do it."

"I don't know. It's ingrained, I guess. I can hear my mother asking me if I'm going to eat anything healthy in the back of my head. So I cave." Karl shrugged and spooned green beans onto his plate. "Tell me about Jamaica."

Adam chewed and tried to organize his thoughts. This was good. Maybe when he was done here, he'd go in and write up his report for the mission committee while it was all fresh in his brain. "Sara Reynolds was there."

Karl frowned and Adam kicked himself. Why had he mentioned her? She wasn't part of the team. She'd been a temporary annoyance—like a mosquito. They'd had plenty of those, too, and yet they weren't the first thing off his tongue.

Karl set his fork down. "I didn't realize she'd signed up. When did that happen?"

"She didn't. She was there on vacation at one of those fancy resorts. I don't know why I mentioned her, we only bumped into each other twice. It was nothing."

"Uh-huh."

"It's true. Anyway, the teens were mostly good. That girl, Melody, was a problem like everyone said she would be. But the guys were pretty good about ignoring her. That surprised me, honestly. She's a cute girl."

Karl shook his head. "Yeah, but she's got a rep. I don't work with the youth all that often and even *I* know about it. A guy hangs with her, he's asking to be painted with that same brush. And they all know that. It's unfair, really. From what I've heard, she's trying—or had been trying—to change and get her life on track. But if she's used to a certain amount of attention and if it all goes away, it's going to be tough."

"So, what, negative attention is better than none? That's dumb."

"Pfft. Please. Even adults are like that, sometimes."

Okay, so maybe that was true. Didn't mean it wasn't dumb. "Still. Sometimes people say they've changed but it's just an act. Take Sara."

Karl's eyebrows lifted. "From everything I've seen, and heard for that matter, she really has turned her life around. It's ticked off several of the guys in the singles group."

"How would you know?"

"I go to the men's breakfasts that you don't. They talk. Loudly."

Adam frowned. If Karl was overhearing it, that meant the pastor was, too. "So why doesn't Pastor Brown do something about it?"

"What's he supposed to do? His messages are always on point. He gives us all the right instruction—but what we do with it is up to us. He can't change someone's heart. Only God can do that."

Back to people changing. "Do you really think God can work in a heart that's hardened toward Him?"

"Um, duh? If He couldn't, no one would ever be saved."

"No. I don't mean the first time—obviously He can call people to Himself. But if you come and then you change your mind, is He really going to waste His time chasing you down again?"

"Waste His time?" Karl shook his head. "Bro, you've never heard of grace?"

Adam sighed. "You ever hear of cheap grace?"

"Okay, sure, once you accept Jesus as your savior, your life should change. But sometimes people slip up—in big or small ways—God still loves them and wants them to return. The Bible's full of stories of exactly that. Honestly, look at the Israelites."

"Yeah, I guess." It just didn't seem right to him.

"What's your issue with Sara anyway?"

Adam shrugged. He didn't feel like getting into it. Karl wouldn't understand. Or he'd say something about repressed attraction. And that was the farthest thing from the truth. He wasn't interested in her in the least. Honestly, if he could go the rest of his life without having to interact with her, he'd consider himself lucky. "Nothing."

"Right." Karl reached into the bucket for another piece of chicken. "It's okay to say you don't want to talk about it."

"There's nothing to talk about." Adam frowned and tipped the bucket so he could see in. "What'd I miss around here?"

5

Sara sighed as her cell phone rang. She'd only been home two hours. Why was anyone calling already? She'd texted to let everyone know she was back safely and that she planned to nap and get organized before work started back up the next day. Now...well, she *could* ignore the call.

Except she couldn't.

Whose number was that, anyway? She swiped to answer it. "Hello?"

"Hi, Sara? This is Pastor Brown from church. Do you have a minute?"

Her stomach clenched. The pastor? She hadn't done anything wrong. In fact, the people at the church in Jamaica had all seemed incredibly pleased with her exercise suggestions. And there was nothing that was going to hurt them. She swallowed. "Sure. Of course."

"I got an email from our sister church earlier today and wanted to know if I could get your email address and forward it along. You did some great work down there this week. It's the closest I've ever seen the pastor down there come to gushing. I thought you'd enjoy reading it. I don't remember seeing your name on the mission team roster, though."

Her cheeks heated. "I wasn't actually there with the team. I ran into some of the group at the falls and then when I tried to attend a Wednesday evening service, one thing led to another. Although I didn't get the impression that my help was particularly welcome."

"Oh? Because the pastor down there..."

"Not from the pastor. He was great. Just Adam Lassiter? I think that's his last name. He was pretty adamant that I should butt out." Sara chewed her lip. She shouldn't have said that. She scrambled to try and cover it. "I think he had good intentions. I wasn't there with them, and I'm not a doctor or anything—he probably didn't want to risk, I don't know, a lawsuit? If something went wrong, that'd be possible, right?"

"Hmm. Well, I appreciate you taking time from your vacation to do something like that. It made a big impression and several of the older folks you helped are already saying they're feeling an improvement. Would you like that email?"

"Yes, I'd love that." She rattled off her email address. Sara smiled. The best part of her job was watching people get better and get back to their lives. Maybe she wouldn't get that in these cases, but knowing she'd made a difference was enough. "Thanks."

"You're very welcome. We're going to be talking about putting together a more medically oriented trip down there in the late spring or early summer. Would you be interested in being part of that?"

Would she? Could she take the time off? Well, she could, but it would mean giving up the idea of another vacation...which wasn't a bad thing necessarily. As much as she loved the beach, being there by herself had been boring. It was fine the first couple of days, but after that? It was no wonder she'd sought out something else to do. "I'm not sure...I mean, I'm just a physical therapist."

Pastor Brown chuckled. "I don't think you need the word 'just' in front of that. It'd probably be a lot like what you did already, showing people exercises and that sort of thing. I'm talking to an orthopedist, and I think I've got him interested. He'd probably appreciate the help you could provide."

"I guess. I just can't believe there's a need, it's not like this is teeth and eyes or basic medicine. But if you think they could use me, I'd be willing to explore the possibility."

"Excellent. I'll put your name on the list and someone from the mission committee will be in touch with more details. But probably not until mid-January. Maybe later."

"Okay. Thanks." Sara ended the call and dropped her phone on the kitchen counter. Was she really going to try a mission trip? That type of thing had never been on her radar before. Why now?

"So tell us everything. Leave no details out." Jen leaned across the table and snagged the salt shaker. "Especially if it involves a cute guy."

"You're engaged. Why are you asking about cute guys?" Sara shook her head and studied her friend. "Are you okay?"

Rebecca pushed the basket of bread closer to the center of the table. "I'm married and still curious about any cute guys. But I also want to hear your answer, Jen."

Jen sighed. "I'm okay. This time of year is hard—it's dark so much and with all the wedding stress...I don't know. Some days it's hard to get out of bed and paste on a smile."

"I thought you'd found the combination of meds that worked for that." Sara frowned. "Have you talked to your doctor?"

"You're as bad as David. I have an appointment next week." Jen pushed the food around on her plate.

"What? That's good, right?" Sara sipped her soda.

"It's just...I want to be fixed, not keep having to adjust and tweak and whatever. Why doesn't God take the depression away permanently?" Jen scrubbed her hands over her face and fixed on a smile. "But that's not why we're here. We're here to listen to you tell us about your Jamaican adventure."

Rebecca reached across the table and laid her hand on Jen's arm. "Are you sure? We can do that another time if you need to talk."

Jen shook her head. "I don't want to. It's all the same stuff. If you're even half as tired of it as I am, you're not interested."

Sara snickered. "We *are* interested. But I also hear what you're saying. First, I'll point out that it was mean of Rebecca not to bring the baby with her. I was counting on getting to hold her."

"Sorry. Ben's still on leave, and Chloe was sleeping so...I was looking forward to a few minutes without her. Next time." Rebecca pointed her fork at Sara. "No more delay tactics. You're making me think there's a good story that you're trying to keep to yourself."

Sara laughed. "Yeah...not so much. Did you know the church had a mission trip headed down there last week?"

"Sure. They asked for chaperone volunteers in class in August. Do you ever listen during announcements?" Jen picked up a fry and dunked it into her ketchup.

"Guess not. Probably will now, though, since I'll be the only one of us left in there. Are you really switching to the young married class already?"

"Sorry. David *hates* the singles class."

Sara couldn't blame him. She didn't love it herself. There weren't really any other options. Oh, she could go to any class, but the handful of times she'd tried, the regular attendees had looked at her like she had three heads and asked if she knew they had a huge singles group. "Anyway, I bumped into them my first day. They were at Dunn River Falls—I guess it was their nod to giving the kids a chance to sightsee so their vacation wasn't all work. Ended up helping with a twisted ankle. Do either of you know Adam Lassiter?"

"Sure. Adam's nice. He does a lot of organizing for the class—anytime there's an outing he's probably in the background making sure it works out. I think he schedules snacks, too. Kinda quiet, though, mostly hangs out with that sturdy girl. What's her name?" Jen looked at Rebecca and pointed a finger. "You know who I mean, right?"

"Sturdy, really?" Rebecca shook her head. "Molly is a beautiful woman inside and out. I tried a number of times to get her to hang out with us, but she never would commit. I thought for a while she and Adam were going to end up together, but last I talked to her that was absolutely off the table. Too bad. They're great friends. I can't help but think that'd make a good match."

Sara snorted. "Lucky escape for her, as far as I'm concerned."

"What?" Jen pushed her barely touched plate away from her. "What happened?"

Sara told them about her interactions with Adam, ending with his accosting her at the resort. She smirked. "But from what I heard yesterday, his little snit backfired on him in a big way. I arranged to help off site so Mr. Superior wouldn't hear about it and make trouble. The local pastor emailed Pastor Brown and now they're working on arranging a more medical trip because I was so helpful."

"Are you going to go?" Jen drew her eyebrows together. "You won't miss my wedding, right?"

"I'm thinking about it. I have a hard time believing they need a physical therapist though. Still, he said late spring or early summer. Your wedding is what, six weeks out?"

Jen groaned. "Don't remind me. I have so much to do between now and then. Whose dumb idea was it to get married on Valentine's Day?"

Rebecca grinned. "Yours. And I think it's incredibly romantic."

Sara chuckled. "I'm with Bec on that. Plus, as a bonus, David's not likely to forget your anniversary."

"That's the idea. Assuming I can get everything organized in time." Jen managed a weak smile.

"What's left to do? Invitations have been mailed—that's the biggie, right?" Sara scraped the last bite off her plate. "Can we help?"

"I...kind of still need a dress."

Rebecca coughed.

"You're not serious." Sara opened and shut her mouth several times as she tried to imagine how Jen had let something like that go for so long. "No wonder you're stressed."

"What happened?" Rebecca pinned Jen with a look that made Sara squirm in sympathy.

Jen looked down and mumbled just loud enough to be heard. "I kept thinking I'd lose some weight...by the time I realized that wasn't going to happen..."

"Okay. So Saturday? We're picking you up at nine and we're not coming home until you have a dress." Sara pulled out her phone and tapped in a reminder. "Rebecca, you're still on maternity leave, make some calls and get appointments where they're needed. Make up an itinerary."

"What's your budget?" Rebecca had her own phone out and was making notes. "Have you at least looked at magazines to know what style you're interested in?"

Jen named a figure.

Sara winced. There wasn't much to work with. "I think there's an outlet in Springfield."

Rebecca nodded. "I got mine there. We can make this happen. I'll meet you at Jen's. Bring coffee."

Sara glanced at her watch and stood. "I need to get back. I've got a full schedule this afternoon. Make a list of anything else you haven't done yet, Jen, we'll talk it over on Saturday."

"Don't think I'm letting this thing with Adam go. He's a nice guy. I want to know why you don't get that." Jen's voice trailed after Sara as she headed toward the restaurant door. She lifted a hand and crossed mental fingers that her friends would take that as an acknowledgment rather than the desperate hope they'd forget about it by the weekend.

6

Adam strode down the hall of the education wing of the church. He was running late. Traffic had been a nightmare. Of course, it was a day ending in "y" here in the D.C. area, so it shouldn't have been a surprise. It just seemed to be worse than usual. And of course he'd been tied up with a client who thought they knew better than everyone.

Molly turned the corner and nearly ran into him. She laughed as she stepped back. "You look awful. Take a breath. They're running late."

"Seriously?" Maybe it was the day for it.

Molly nodded. "I was going out to my car to find my phone and let you know."

"Why is your phone in your car?" He was lost without his cell. Leaving it at home for the week-long mission trip had probably been good for him. But as soon as he'd gotten back, that puppy went right back in his pocket.

"Didn't need it for this." She grinned. "And some of us manage to avoid the addiction. So...the youth group is running late because the Wednesday night dinner ran over. What's your excuse?"

Dinner. He'd missed that, too. How had he forgotten that was this week? He always looked forward to the semi-monthly meals at church when a large portion of those who attended got together for a meal of chicken and salad. The food wasn't amazing, but it gave him a chance to talk to people who he'd otherwise never see in a church this big. Adam sighed. "Client who thinks he can build houses better than me and has to second guess everything. Right now, he's convinced that the architect has added unnecessary supports just to increase materials costs. Honestly, if we hadn't already started digging the foundation, I'd be tempted to hand his check back and apologize for the scheduling error that made it impossible for us to fit him in."

Molly snickered. "Except you wouldn't do that, even if you could. I know you."

He shrugged. "You're probably right. Although...I swear this is going to take twice as long to finish because of his interference. I'll be glad to see the back of him."

"And when he has a house by Lassiter, he'll never need to bother another builder again."

Adam laughed. "I'll put your advertising check in the mail. Although I guess I'd prefer you wait until you're talking to someone who's looking to buy a house. Buttering me up has no purpose."

"Maybe I'm just trying to cheer you up."

"You've succeeded. Why aren't we dating again?"

Molly made a gagging motion. "Because I don't date my siblings. And while it's true we're not biologically related, we might as well be. Blech. Don't even kid. I don't need to throw up when it's time to talk about the trip."

Even though he agreed with her, his ego took the hit squarely on the nose and he clutched his chest. "Ouch. Maybe it's because you've got a mean streak."

Shaking her head, Molly started toward the youth room. "If it helps you sleep better at night, you go ahead and believe that. Come on. They'll be ready for us in about five."

He followed her into the classroom. There were at least fifty teens seated in rows facing the front of the room. The youth pastor was in the middle of what was probably his mini lesson. Adam scooted along the back wall with Molly, trying to make as little noise as possible.

Before long, the youth pastor segued into the importance of sharing Jesus' love with everyone the kids met and called the mission team to the front of the room. Some of the kids looked distinctly uncomfortable, while others—like Melody—were practically preening. Adam fought the urge to roll his eyes. There'd been girls like her when he'd been in youth group, too. Some things never seemed to go out of style.

Everyone took a minute or two to talk about what they liked and what they learned during their week in Jamaica. Adam's heart swelled a little as some of the guys mentioned their evening Bible studies and one-on-one talks they'd had with him. Maybe he'd made a difference to more than just the people they'd travelled to help. Did he have time to volunteer more frequently with the youth? He'd have to pray about it.

When they'd finished, Adam aimed for a seat in the back of the room. Maybe he'd hang out for the rest of the evening and see what volunteering looked like. He'd helped out on retreats when they needed more chaperones, and the mission trip of course, but what was really involved on a weekly basis?

"Adam, right?"

The pastor was here, too? Adam nodded. "Yes, sir."

Pastor Brown grinned. "Could we chat in the hall a minute?"

"Of course." Adam followed the pastor into the hall, squashing the questions that flashed through his mind.

"I'm glad I was able to sit in on the report. Sounds like everyone had a productive and meaningful trip. I've already had a few communications with the pastor down there—he's very appreciative of all the hard work the team put in. And the help that came from outside the team."

Adam frowned. Outside the team? "I'm glad to hear that. I've been feeling like God might be calling me to ministry in some way...this trip solidified some of that."

"Hmm. Would you consider going back in the late spring or summer? The next trip is going to be primarily medical in nature, but you're a builder, right?"

Adam nodded.

"There's always a construction project or two that needs doing."

"When will there be more details about the timeline? Getting away isn't always easy, so it'd depend on the state my projects are in." Adam tucked his hands in his pockets and tried to remember what new contracts were under review. But that's why he had an electronic calendar and to-do list. His memory wasn't something he cared to rely on.

"Probably the end of the month. You don't have a problem with the medical focus?" The pastor was watching him carefully. Did Adam have something on his face?

"No. Why would I?"

"I'm not sure. I'd just heard that you weren't supportive of that type of aid on this last trip. Maybe I was mistaken."

Adam's jaw dropped. Sara Reynolds. Of course. "I'm not sure what you heard, but there was another woman from the church who wasn't part of the mission team down there. She helped out with a twisted ankle on our touring day, which was great, but then she took it on herself to dole out medical advice at the Wednesday night service and it was starting to snowball. I just suggested that since she's not a doctor she should probably hold off on practicing medicine without a license."

Pastor Brown tapped the fingers of one hand on his leg. "The physical therapy clinic she did was well received and quite helpful for a number of the congregants down there. They're hoping to be able to reach outside the church next time. Sometimes people won't come to a church to hear about Jesus, but they'll come if it'll help their bodies feel better."

Adam's neck burned. His cheeks were probably bright red as well. "Of course. Maybe the next trip isn't a great fit for me, then. Thanks for the information."

"Adam." The pastor's voice held compassion as well as steel.

He stopped and turned. "Yes?"

"I think you probably owe her an apology. Don't you?"

Adam paced outside the sanctuary. After Pastor Brown's talk, he hadn't felt like going back in with the youth. Nothing quite like getting called on the carpet to get your nerves jangling. There was no way he could sit still. He'd thought maybe popping into the prayer meeting would help him settle. Except, of course, that he'd spotted Sara the instant before he pulled open the door.

An apology.

The worst part was that the pastor was right. He would probably have come to that conclusion on his own eventually. Or Molly would've pointed it out. His gut twisted. Better to get it over with now rather than putting it off. Then he could focus on figuring out if this next mission trip was something he should try to be part of. Would Sara really be going? That...made it less likely that he should even consider it. How could someone with her past be an asset in reaching others for Jesus?

The piano started to play, and the doors opened. He took a deep breath. He'd find her, say he was sorry, and move on. That would be the end of it.

Adam scanned the clumps of people as they exited. Wouldn't it be just his luck if she went out another door? Then he'd have to find her number and call her. She'd probably get the wrong idea. Or refuse to pick up. Acid burned the back of his throat. A flicker of color caught his eye and he turned. There she was.

He pushed through the crowd. "Sara."

She stopped and turned. The puzzled look on her face morphed into a stony one when her gaze landed on him. "What?"

"Do you have a minute?" Adam fought the urge to put his hands in his pockets. Or cross his arms.

"For?"

He cleared his throat. Maybe it was better to just spit it out here, in front of everyone, rather than try to get her to go someplace more private. "I wanted to apologize for my behavior in Jamaica."

Her eyebrows lifted.

Great. She was one of those people who made you spell it out in minute detail. Of course she was. "So. I'm sorry for what I said. I hope you'll forgive me."

Sara tilted her head to the side and studied him before nodding slowly. "Thank you."

"All right. Well. Have a good night." Now Adam did put his hands in his pockets. That was done. And not as painful as it could have been. Did he need to tell Pastor Brown, or was it enough that he'd followed through? He turned and started toward his car. Surely, the pastor had better things to worry about.

"Adam?"

Now what? He stopped and looked over his shoulder.

Sara closed the distance between them. "I didn't manage to get here in time for the church dinner, so I thought I'd run across the street and have Chinese. You wouldn't maybe want to join me, would you?"

That would be no. Big, huge, fat no. Why would he possibly want to eat dinner with her? "Sure."

She sent him a bright smile. "Really? Cool. You want to meet over there? Save another trip across that crazy road?"

"Yeah, that works. I'll see you there." He turned and strode through the foyer and out into the parking lot. When he got to his car, his head dropped to the steering wheel. He'd lost his mind. There was no other possible explanation. He reached for his phone and dialed Karl. His roommate picked up on the second ring. "Hey man, if I'm not home in two hours, call the cops. My last known will be the Chinese place across from church."

Karl laughed. "Ooookay. Gonna explain any more than that?"

"No. I don't think you'd believe me."

"I'll just make stuff up then. Let's see...you're going on a date with Sara Reynolds."

Adam shook his head and clicked his seatbelt into place.

"I was kidding."

"Yeah, well...I'm not. Although I don't think she considers it a date. I know I don't." Adam turned on the car and backed out of his space.

Karl's laughter filled the car. "Oh, man. That's rich. I want details."

"There aren't going to be details. Unless, of course, she stabs me in the eye with a chopstick and hides the body somewhere. Two hours. I'm serious." Adam zipped across the busy two-lane road and into the turn lane that led to the shopping center across from the church.

"Got it. I still want deets when you get home."

"If I get home." Adam punched end before Karl could laugh himself sick again. He really needed to do a web search on sudden-onset insanity...when he got home.

7

Sara waved to Adam from the booth where she'd been seated. This was the only Chinese restaurant in the area that she knew of where you could actually sit inside and eat. Well, except for the super fancy one in Tyson's Corner. Most of the others were takeout or delivery only. She still wasn't quite sure why she'd asked Adam to join her.

"Thanks for coming. I don't mind eating alone, but I always feel like they're waiting for me to leave when I do."

Adam chuckled and slid onto the bench opposite her. "I've never even tried. I always just call in an order from the parking lot and wait until it's ready. It's...very pink."

Sara grinned. The light pink decor on the walls and upholstery never went with Chinese food in her mind. "Yeah. But the food makes up for it. And honestly, it's...kind of quaint."

"Fair enough." Adam reached for the pot of tea that the waitress deposited on their table and flipped over the small, handleless cups. "Tea?"

Sara shrugged. She didn't usually bother. She had to dump so much sugar into it to make it palatable, but he was trying to be nice, so... "Sure."

He filled the cups and reached for a sugar packet.

"You are ready to order?" The tiny woman in a silk dress stopped at their table, the pad and pen completely out of place with the elegance of her outfit.

"I am. Adam?"

He nodded.

"Okay. I'd like the Kung Pao chicken, please. And some water."

Adam pursed his lips. "The same, with an egg roll."

The woman nodded and disappeared into the back.

The silence at the table was awkward. Had she made a mistake asking him to come? She wouldn't have if Jen and Rebecca hadn't been so adamant yesterday that he was a nice guy. And he did apologize. "So. Tell me about yourself."

"There's not much to tell. I have a building company with my brothers. We do custom houses and some remodeling, though that aspect of our business hasn't really taken off yet. When I'm not doing that, I'm either at church or playing soccer." He winced. "I sound boring."

Sara laughed. "No, you don't. I don't know that there's a way to answer that question without it coming out like that."

"Let's test that theory. Your turn."

"My turn? To...oh." She shook her head. "Got it. And you're right. It's a terrible question. I'm making a mental note to never ask it again. Unless it's a job interview. Maybe not even then."

Adam grinned. "You're stalling."

"I'm trying not to sound boring." She took a deep breath and wiped sweaty palms on her jeans. "Let's see. I'm a physical therapist, which you know. Contrary to what you seem to think, it does actually require a graduate degree and while, no, it's not medical school, it was still a rigorous program with a dissertation and licensing exams afterward. Um. Outside of work, I spend a lot of time hanging out with friends...though they're all married or engaged at this point so maybe I should think about a hobby. I've always wanted to learn to ice skate."

"Ice skate. Like twirling and stuff?" He cocked his head to the side. "I can kind of see that."

She shook her head. Why had she mentioned skating? No one knew about that. Or about her secret fascination with figure skating movies. And what did it say about him that he didn't look even the tiniest bit ashamed by her mention of her doctorate? She was saved from asking by the arrival of the food.

"Can I pray?"

Her eyebrows lifted. She'd figured they'd both pray on their own. She nodded.

He stretched his arm across the table and held out his hand.

Swallowing hard, she rested her fingers in his. The electricity was still there. Sara closed her eyes and tried to concentrate on his words and not the tingles that simply proved that chemistry didn't mean anything. If there were two more incompatible people in the world, she didn't know them. It was too bad, really. He was attractive and maybe even fun. When he wasn't being a jerk.

"Why didn't either of you tell me you weren't going to be at church on Wednesday?" Sara glanced at Jen in the rearview mirror before looking at Rebecca in the passenger seat. "You could have saved me from myself."

"Uh oh. What'd you do now?" Jen leaned forward and rested her elbows on the front seats.

"I asked Adam to dinner after prayer meeting."

"Adam?" Jen frowned.

"Adam Lassiter?" Rebecca laughed. "I don't believe it for a second. Turn here."

Sara sighed and turned into the strip mall parking lot and started hunting for a spot near the discount bridal store. "Believe it or not, it's true."

"Back up and start from the beginning. There's one on the left." Jen pointed.

Sara turned the wheel and eased into the parking space. She shifted into park and turned off the engine. "There's not a lot to tell. He cornered me after prayer meeting and apologized for what he said in Jamaica. I accepted. And then, before I realized what I was doing, I'd asked him to have Chinese across the street."

"And he said yes." Rebecca gathered a fat folder from the floor of the car and grinned. "So...how was it?"

Jen pushed open her door with a grin. "What she said. And did you get the Kung Pao again or actually try something new and also delicious?"

"Why mess with a good thing?" Sara shrugged. She liked the Kung Pao chicken. It wasn't like she ate there so often she needed to branch out and try another dish. When she wanted Chinese, she wanted spicy chicken with peanuts. If that wasn't what she was in the mood for, she didn't bother with Chinese. It was a simple—straightforward even—system. Why couldn't her friends get that?

Rebecca shook her head and tugged open the door to the shop.

"Can I help you ladies?" An older woman manned a small table just inside the door. Beyond her, racks of white and cream dresses lined the massive space. Clumps of women roamed up and down them, stopping occasionally to pull out a plastic-covered gown and squeal.

"We have an appointment. The bride is Jen Andrews." Rebecca reached back and dragged Jen forward.

The woman consulted the book in front of her and smiled. "Of course. You'll be working with Sienna. She's finishing up with another client and should be free in about ten minutes. If you want to browse while you wait, you can do that, or I can get you set up in a fitting room."

"We'll browse. Thanks." Sara smiled and pointed to the far end of the room where the crowds were thinner. "Let's start down there."

Rebecca growled. "I was thinking we could sit and wait. Why are we browsing when Jen doesn't know what she wants yet?"

"I don't even know why we're shopping when I haven't figured that out." Jen crossed her arms.

"Oh please. You're not going to figure it out if you don't look. Come on. You know the basics, right? Long sleeves and white, right?"

Jen sighed. "Yeah. Sleeveless is not for me. I can pull off white, right? I don't have to go with cream?"

Rebecca pursed her lips and studied Jen. "Yeah. I think you can swing it. But maybe we should try some of each just in case. Sleeves, though, that may be harder. Still, there are probably a few in here that aren't strapless. Surely one or two designers take pity on people who don't want to risk having their dresses fall off while they walk down the aisle."

"Okay." Jen looked at the packed rack of dresses. "Where do you even start?"

"You still a ten?" Sara walked halfway down the rack to where a plastic tab with the number ten poked up above the offerings.

Rebecca pushed a dress back in and strode down to where Sara was. "I forgot they had them arranged by size. Why do you remember?"

Sara shrugged. She'd spent enough time here with Rebecca last year, it shouldn't be a surprise. She pushed the dresses down the bar and eyed the first in the section. "What do you think of this?"

"From what I can see, I like it." Jen reached for the dress. "Can we pull it out?"

"Let's just take it with us and when we get that fitting room, you can see it all while you try it on." Sara lifted the dress off the rack and studied the next one. Sequins, crystals, and bead pearls covered nearly every inch of the bodice. "This is too glitzy, I think?"

Jen nodded. "Maybe this won't be as dreadful as I thought it would be."

Rebecca laughed. "There's your optimism coming out again."

They worked their way through three racks of dresses before Sienna came to get them. "Wow. You've already pulled quite a few. You're making my job easy."

"It seemed like a better idea than just sitting around." Jen clutched the stack of dresses. "It's okay, right?"

"Absolutely. Come on this way and we'll get you started trying things on. Do you want your friends to go in with you or wait out by the mirrors?" Sienna talked over her shoulder as she led them through a door at the back of the store that opened to a space almost the same size as the front. Changing rooms lined the long wall separating this area from the main part of the store and six raised circles surrounded on three sides with mirrors filled the rest. A handful of chairs grouped around each of the pedestals.

"Um." Jen glanced between Sara and Rebecca.

"We'll wait out here." Sara pointed to an empty viewing space. "This one okay?"

Sienna nodded. "Of course. Have you thought about undergarments at all?"

Jen shook her head.

"All right. Let's take a look at the dresses you've got and I'll make some recommendations." Sienna smiled at Sara and Rebecca. "Make yourselves at home, ladies. We won't be long."

"You managed to sidestep nicely when we arrived, but now you don't have any excuse. I need more details about this dinner with Adam." Rebecca settled into one of the chairs and dropped her purse at her feet.

"It was nothing. Just dinner." Sara sat and wriggled until she found a comfortable position. They could spend a little more on their chairs if they wanted people to enjoy helping someone shop. Or maybe that was the point. If the chairs were horrid, the entourage wouldn't want to linger, and maybe decisions would get made faster.

"So no conversation?"

"Please. We didn't sit there in silence. But it wasn't anything earth shattering, either." Though it had been pleasant. Adam was funny. And easy to look at. Not that that erased his treatment of her in Jamaica. Although he had apologized.

"Hmm."

"There's no 'hmm.' We had dinner and a reasonably pleasant conversation and I'm now prepared to agree with you that it seems like he might be a nice guy. Happy?" Why had she even brought up the dinner in the first place?

"Did you notice he's good looking?" Rebecca waggled her eyebrows.

Sara sighed. "I'm not blind, okay? Besides, I'm pretty sure I mentioned that the first time he came up in conversation."

"Right. When you thought he was a jerk."

Sara nodded.

"Has that changed?"

Had it? She'd had all of three conversations with the guy. One was...she'd call it neutral. One absolutely hostile. And one pleasant. How did that average out? "Yeah, I guess."

Rebecca grinned. "Are you going to see him again?"

"I'm sure he'll be at church. Maybe he'll say hi now." Sara looked over her shoulder at the closed changing room door. How long did it take to get into a wedding dress?

"Sara."

"What?"

"Do you like him?"

Sara shrugged. "Maybe a little. The real question is whether he's even remotely interested. Because he's hard to read. For now, I'm content to let it alone. I'm not sure I'm ready to date anyone anyway."

"Luc still?" Rebecca frowned. "You need to forgive yourself and move on."

"I'm working on it."

The door to the changing room opened, and Jen stepped out. The skirt was a fullish A-line and the delicately beaded bodice fit like it had been custom made for her. Delicate three-quarter length lace sleeves added a touch of modesty without making the dress feel old fashioned.

"You look amazing." Rebecca reached out to straighten the short train once Jen stood on the platform. "Is this the first one?"

Jen nodded. "I'm kind of thinking it's the last, too. It's perfect."

Sienna grinned. "I think you should try on the others, but this certainly gets things off to a good start."

Sara leaned back in her chair and watched Jen swivel to see the various angles of the dress. Maybe today wasn't going to be nearly as awful as she'd expected.

8

Molly's elbow jammed into his ribs and she spoke in a whisper. "There she is."

"Who?" Adam frowned and slipped his phone back into his pocket. There wasn't supposed to be any work happening on any of the job sites today. Lassiter Brothers didn't work on Sunday. Period. That had been one of the first things Adam and his brothers, Aaron and Asher, had emphasized when they decided to go into business. And yet he'd been getting texts from two different subcontractors all morning. Why was it so hard for them to read the timeline he'd emailed out last week and see that he'd already clearly fixed the scheduling conflict that they'd created by leaving one another out of the loop?

"Sara. She looks nice this morning, too."

Before he could stop himself, Adam followed Molly's nod and his gaze landed on Sara sitting by herself in the back row with a cup of coffee and her phone in her lap. She did look nice. But then, when didn't she? It was just proof that the outside packaging could be amazing and still hide a nightmare. His conscience twinged. She hadn't seemed like a nightmare on Wednesday. In fact, he'd had the best time he'd had hanging out with a girl who wasn't Molly in...forever. He still shouldn't have mentioned that to Molly. "Hmm."

"Really?" Molly's eyes bored into him. "You said you had a good time. That she was interesting and nice. Do you remember this conversation?"

Heat crawled up his neck. "Yeah. So?"

"So go say hello. Offer to sit with her."

"I always sit with you."

Molly rolled her eyes. "It's not a law, you know. You can sit wherever you want. With whomever you want."

"Listen to you, 'whomever.' Your grandmother would be proud."

Molly laughed. "My grandmother would probably be chastising me for being pretentious. Or, as she called it, too big for my britches. And you're not dodging this. Do you, or do you not, want to get to know Sara better?"

That was the million-dollar question. On the one hand, if he could go based on their interactions on Wednesday, yeah, he did. But he knew so much more about her past, and it made him pause. "I don't know."

"You're not still hung up on her past, are you?" Molly shook her head. "Who do you think you are to hold that over her when Jesus has forgiven her, and it's clear she's made changes in her lifestyle?"

"How do we know they're permanent?" Adam stared across the room and quickly looked away when Sara glanced up and caught him.

"Pfft. 'Cause you never sin."

He sighed. "I don't want her to get the wrong idea."

"Which is what? That you think she's interesting and worth getting to know?"

How did Molly manage to twist his words like that? "Fine. I'll go see if I can sit with her. Happy?"

"Delirious. You want me to come?"

He fought the urge to scream. "Seriously? After all that, you're going to come too?"

Molly smirked. "Not like I have anyone else to sit with. Besides, we always sit together."

"Come on, then. Let's go get seats before everything starts." Adam's phone buzzed in his pocket again. He ignored it. They didn't work on Sunday. The subs should know this.

"I'll be there in a minute, I need a refill." Molly wiggled her coffee cup.

Sure she did. But whatever. Adam tucked his hands into his pockets then pulled them out again. He crossed and uncrossed his arms before giving himself a firm mental shake and crossing the room. His palms were damp. "Hi, Sara."

Sara looked up from her phone and smiled. "Adam."

That wasn't quite the warm welcome he'd expected. Expected? Hoped for, anyway. He cleared his throat. "I was wondering if I could sit with you?"

Her eyebrows lifted but she gestured to the empty chairs on either side of her. "Of course. Although you should know association with me may land you in the pariah camp."

He frowned. She wasn't a pariah. "You have lots of friends."

"Had. Well, I still have a few. But they've all moved to the married classes. Look, I'll understand if you don't want to be guilty by association." She offered a thin smile.

Adam shook his head and plopped into the chair next to her. "I'll risk it. How was the rest of your week?"

"Okay. Look...what is this?" Sara let out a breath and clicked off her phone. "You always sit with Molly. Half the class expects you to get married in the next three months. The other half thinks it might take six. And as much as I enjoyed dinner on Wednesday, I know what you think of me. You've made that clear. So you don't have to do this."

She'd enjoyed dinner. His heart lifted, though he couldn't pinpoint exactly why it mattered. "Molly and I are friends. I think she's half in love with my roommate, to be honest. Though I'm not sure he knows she's a girl."

Sara snorted. "Guys are so oblivious."

"Hey. I resemble that remark." He grinned at her. The corners of her mouth lifted slightly. "As for the rest, I apologized for how I behaved in Jamaica. Maybe you could extend that to anything else I've done to make you think I dislike you?"

After a moment, Sara nodded. "All right. For the record, I'm not proud of the things I did. But I'm also not going to sew a big red

'A' on my clothes. It seems like those are the only two options people expect from me. And I'm serious, if you hang out with me too long, you're going to get painted with the same brush."

Adam shook his head. He couldn't—wouldn't—believe that. The people here knew him. And while sure, he struggled with Sara's history of sleeping around, maybe Molly wasn't wrong either. Before he could speak, the pastor clapped his hands at the front of the room to get started. As Adam pulled out his phone to look up the Bible reading for their lesson, he caught a few sideways glances aimed their way. Well, let them look. He'd worry about that later.

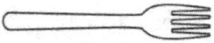

"So I guess the whole 'I never want to interact with her again in my whole life' speech was more of a show than reality?" Karl grinned and offered a game controller to Adam.

Adam groaned. He'd managed to avoid going into detail about his dinner with Sara on Wednesday, but there was no hiding...anything...when he sat with her in Sunday school. "Yeah, I guess. Look, the pastor mentioned that he thought I owed her an apology. He probably wasn't wrong. I did that on Wednesday, we talked for a bit, and...she might actually make an interesting friend."

"An interesting, *attractive* friend." Karl waggled his eyebrows.

"I'll introduce you." Adam's stomach twisted. Maybe he shouldn't have had that sixth piece of pizza at lunch.

"Ha. No thanks. I've got my eye on someone. I'm almost ready to make a move." Karl shrugged. "So the path's clear as far as I'm concerned."

Adam shook his head. He wasn't going to ask who Karl had his eye on. If it wasn't Molly, he'd help pick up the pieces like he usually did when Karl started dating someone. And if it was...well, he wasn't the best at keeping secrets. Especially not from her. He wasn't going to be the one to ruin Karl's surprise.

"That's a long silence over there with nothing happening here in the game."

Adam blew out a breath and hit the button to join. "Sorry."

"Uh huh. When are you asking her out?"

"I don't plan to. Maybe we can be friends, but that's it." It had to be, didn't it? The more he prayed about it, the more he believed that God was calling him into ministry. He wasn't sure, yet, how that was going to work with the building company he and his brothers owned...but maybe there was a way to blend the two. No matter how that worked out, it wasn't likely he'd be able to provide the kind of comfort and luxury Sara was no doubt used to. "Did you hear anything about a second trip to Jamaica?"

Karl shook his head. "Nope. Already itching to go back? You really do have the mission bug, don't you?"

Adam lifted a shoulder. "I like knowing I helped people."

"You know there are ways to do that here, right? There's Habitat for Humanity and all kind of other agencies who would love to use your building know-how."

"Yeah. I haven't figured out how to meld what I do with this nudge I'm feeling to ministry. I don't even know if I'm supposed to. Maybe I should be looking at going to seminary or something else entirely." Adam frowned and opened his in-game inventory to look for a better weapon. It was all so confusing. Here he thought God was calling him one way...but where were the specifics? And how did a friendship—or more?—with Sara factor in? No. She wasn't part of his future. Maybe they could be friends. Or maybe she was some kind of test to see if he was easily distracted from what God really wanted for him.

"This isn't like you. Usually you're the one with a clear plan, taking steps to implement it before everyone else realizes what you're doing."

"I know." That was part of the problem. "I'm not sure what to do...just keep praying about it, I guess. I have to believe that God will make it clear at some point."

Karl grunted. "And Sara?"

His roommate was like a dog with a bone. "That too, I guess."

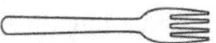

Adam took a long swig of coffee as he stared at the building site. After all the texts during church, he'd anticipated a problem. But this...he shook his head and dialed the plumber.

"Hi, Adam."

"Will. Any chance of an explanation? What I'm seeing here looks like about twenty steps back from where we left it on Friday."

"Don't blame me, man. It's that electrician you hired. He called from the job site on Saturday, said he had to redo the wiring in the basement and was gonna have to tear out some of the plumbing to do it."

"Wiring shouldn't have anything to do with pipes."

"I know that. You know that. Probably anyone with half a brain knows that. But that guy...I dropped everything and headed over, but the damage was done."

Why would the guy cut through pipes? Adam touched the main drain that had been sawed open and sighed. "How soon can you get this fixed?"

"Is that yahoo done?"

"Oh, he's done." On so many levels. This client was already difficult. At least up until now, all the delays weren't the fault of Adam or his team. Now? It was going to be ugly.

Will chuckled. "I like the sound of that. When you've got the electrical figured, give me a call. I'll make you a priority."

"Thanks, man. I appreciate it." Adam ended the call and scrolled through his contacts for the electrician's number. Before he could hit send, his phone rang. He frowned at the number, his finger hovering over the ignore button. He didn't make up his mind fast enough and the call went to voice mail. Well, that saved him making a decision.

He dialed the electrician and waited as it rang, tapping his fingers on his leg. When the call went to voice mail, he frowned and waited for the beep. "Hi, this is Adam Lassiter. I'm standing in the basement of the Folsom Hill project and...there are no words. I'm not sure exactly what you think you're doing, but I can tell you one thing you aren't doing is working for us any longer. And you can be sure that, if asked, I'll be explaining this little hiccup to others in the field who might be stupid enough to hire you. Once I know how much it's going to cost to fix the mess you made, I'll deduct that from what we owe you and send out a payment. Or, more likely, an invoice. Call me if you have any questions."

He took a deep breath and squeezed the back of his neck. Might as well check the message and see if that was more insanity. He had two other jobs to get to today. And he apparently needed to find a new electrician.

"Hi, Adam. This is Sara. Reynolds? I hope it's okay I got your number. I know you do construction and...it's kind of complicated. Maybe you could call me back? I can't usually get to my phone during the day, so after six? 'K. Bye."

Why was his heart racing? Probably still vestiges of the electrical debacle. Had to be. It couldn't be because Sara had called him, no matter what his roommate hinted at. He wasn't interested in her. And she wasn't interested in him. It was a work call—she'd basically said so herself. How many people from church happened across his number when they needed a plumber or a drywall contractor or any other building related serviceperson? Too many to count. He didn't mind passing along contacts when he could. Of course, he wouldn't be passing on this electrician.

Adam sighed. Better to focus on the current problems and sort out whatever Sara needed when she could talk. He glanced at his watch as the drywall crew stomped down the basement stairs. Just about ten hours before he could call back. For now, he had to figure out how to juggle the schedule to factor in redoing the electrical and the plumbing repairs. "Hey guys, we're not going to be down here today. Major issue over the weekend. Head on up and we'll look at the timeline."

9

Sara toed off her shoes and sighed. The carpet was cool and soft on her overtired feet. The office had been hopping today. With Rebecca still out on maternity leave—would she come back?—they were understaffed. It didn't help that the new receptionist had tried to be helpful and ended up double booking several of the day's appointments.

Her stomach growled. Dinner was definitely the first order of business. And then...maybe a movie. There was never anything good on TV anyway. She wasn't going to think about whether or not Adam would call her back.

She stared into the refrigerator and frowned at the contents. Everything in there required more effort than she was ready to put into a meal after the day she'd had. She grabbed a yogurt and the bag of baby carrots in the crisper. Good enough.

Her phone rang as she settled on the couch and reached for the remote. Barely managing to avoid tipping over the yogurt, she swiped accept. "Hello?"

"Hi, Sara. It's Adam? You left me a voicemail this morning?"

She smiled. He sounded nervous. It wasn't a mindset she would ever have ascribed to him. Sara licked yogurt off her finger and set her meal, such as it was, on the coffee table. "Yeah, hi. Thanks for calling back."

"Sure. What can I do for you?"

Where to start. She blew out a breath. "It's kind of a long story. You have a few minutes?"

"Yeah, I'm not doing anything tonight. My roommate's out somewhere. So...?"

"Who's your roommate again?"

"Karl. You know Karl—everyone knows Karl."

Sara laughed. "You're right. Everyone knows Karl. Is he that loud at home?"

"Not usually." Adam chuckled. "But I also have good headphones. He's a good guy. And aside from being a prankster, pretty easy to live with."

Ugh. Pranks. Yet another reason to be grateful she was able to avoid the whole roommate situation. "Huh. Anyway, do you know Rebecca Fischer—er, Taylor?"

"Yeah, sure. A little. She's been married what, a year now? And they have a new baby, right?"

"Right. She's adorable. I'm off track again, sorry. So, there are there are nine of us who usually get together for lunch on Sundays. Not all of us make every week—Jackson and Paige will often go to his sister's house or Zach and Amy don't feel like the trek out of D.C., point being though that we hang out. It's nice. Um. So on Sunday, Rebecca was talking about the homeless mission where she volunteers and how they've just been able to buy the building next door. I guess they're planning to turn it into bigger dorms, maybe even have some short term residency opportunities as people work to get back on their feet."

"Good for them. I've seen the reports on their ministry in the bulletin. And don't they bring muffins to the foyer and sell them sometimes?"

"Yeah, that's them. It's one of their fundraising efforts that combines with job training that they offer as well. So, the new building is...not in good shape. And Rebecca and Ben were talking about options and it occurred to me that maybe this was a place here at home where you could help. I don't even know if you have time— but I'm pretty sure they'd welcome anything you could do." Sara pressed her lips together as silence stretched over the phone. Had she overstepped?

"That's...a really interesting idea."

Sara exhaled, trying to keep it as quiet as she could. "Cool. I can send you some contact info, if you want."

"Yeah. That'd be good. Do you have my email?"

"No. Hang on and I'll get a pen." She moved the carrots out of the way and grabbed an out of date magazine and a pen from the coffee table. "Okay, shoot."

Adam slowly spelled out his email address and Sara read it back to him.

"That's it. Thanks. I'm glad you thought of me."

Thinking of him had been about all she'd been able to do for the last couple of days. Which was stupid and ridiculous. "Me too."

"So. Will you be at church on Wednesday?"

"I usually try to get to prayer meeting. It's a good midweek boost. And I like the time at the end where everyone gets a chance to pray aloud if they want. It feels...special. Holy, somehow. You know?"

"I haven't actually gone before. The class has a Bible study on Wednesdays that I've been going to. What made you choose prayer meeting over that?"

Sara's cheeks burned and her skin prickled as she remembered her one trial of the study. Her voice hardened. "I tried the Bible study in May...ish. They made it clear that while no one had a problem with me trolling for dates in Sunday school, the Bible study was for serious Christians."

"I...wow. I'm sorry."

"It wasn't you." She took a deep breath and held it while she counted to five before letting it out. "Doesn't matter. Turns out that prayer meeting is amazing, and I'm glad I'm not missing out on that. It's an older crowd, though Jen, David, Rebecca, and Ben try to come too, usually. The pastor does a little devotion and then it's just time to pray for one another. Sometimes little groups form, sometimes not. But I always leave refreshed. It's helped me see prayer in a whole new life and my personal prayer life is better for it."

Adam cleared his throat. "Would it be okay if I joined you?"

"Sure, it's open to anyone." She scooped a bite of yogurt.

"No. I didn't mean...you know what, that's good. I may see you then. Hopefully I'll have some details on this project. Have a good night. And eat something other than carrots."

She laughed. "Sorry. They're loud."

"It's okay. Good night."

"Night." Sara ended the call and pressed a hand to her quivering belly. It was hunger. Couldn't possibly be anything else. Could it?

Sara darted into the sub shop next to the medical office building where she worked. Jen was already at one of the tables with a salad and soda in front of her. "Sorry I'm late. Let me order and I'll be right there."

Thankfully, there wasn't a line. Most people were finished with lunch by one-thirty in the afternoon. Sara shook her head as she pointed to the toppings she wanted on her sandwich. Rebecca had officially given her notice that she wasn't returning to work after her maternity leave was up. Everyone was panicking. Hopefully they'd be able to hire one—or two—new therapists.

With her sandwich and a bottle of juice in hand, she crossed to Jen's table and flopped into a chair. "Thanks for making the trip out. And for waiting. I know it's late."

Jen shrugged. "I didn't have anything going on this afternoon that can't wait a little. David's in a meeting that goes through lunch, and probably dinner if his texts are any indication. So, what's up?"

"I'm over thinking a phone call. Or I'm over thinking about over thinking. Or something. I need help." Sara took a bite of her sandwich and tried to organize her thoughts. "Adam."

"Oh yeah?" Jen brightened. "I was hoping something might happen with him. Leave out no details."

"Nothing's happening. I'm still pretty sure I'm not dating anyone." Possibly ever again. Even if that twisted her heart and popped dreams she'd held tightly to since she was a little girl. She'd given that part of her life to God, and she wasn't going to take it back. Not when she'd messed it up so badly already. "Anyway, that's kind of the problem. I got the sense maybe he was flirting? I don't know what to do."

"What's to know? He's a good looking, single Christian man. You flirt back."

"Jen. You know me. You know the train wreck I make of things."

"In the past. That last word's the important one." Jen stabbed her salad. "Look, there's no question you made bad choices. But you're not alone in having made those. Every guy you hooked up with was in the singles class."

"Not every guy." Sara prodded the bread of her sub, her appetite gone. "Not Luc."

"No, but he said he was a believer. Maybe even really feels that's true. Do you remember sitting in the hot tub at Rebecca's complex, telling us all how outdated and unrealistic it was to think it was possible to stay a virgin until you were married?"

Heat burned her cheeks and her stomach twisted. "Yeah."

Jen pointed a finger at her. "You're not alone in thinking that. How many people are there who claim Christ but still go on to justify a pet sin in the name of being loving or having to modernize with the times?"

Sara shrugged.

"A lot. Let's just go with that. Which means there are a lot of people who have made mistakes. And yet, if they turn back to God and truly repent—meaning they stop doing what they were doing and strive to live in the Spirit—like you've done—then it's not for us to continue to condemn them. Which means you need to forgive yourself."

Forgive herself? "That's not—I have."

"Have you? Really?" Jen took a bite.

Of course she had. Sara furrowed her brow. "Why would you say I haven't?"

"Because it seems to be a frequent excuse for why you can't live a normal life and do things like flirt with a cute guy who's apparently interested in you."

"How come you have all the answers?"

Jen grinned. "I go to a lot of therapy."

It was good that it wasn't a church dinner night. Sara wouldn't have been able to keep anything down. She'd barely managed to finish her sandwich with Jen and had spent the whole afternoon with her thoughts scattered. Adam wasn't her type, was he? Even if he was, was she his? Maybe she'd read too much into...everything. With a deep breath, she sat in a pew and forced herself to look straight ahead. She wasn't going to get caught staring at the doors waiting for him to arrive. There was no way for that to turn out well.

"Hey. Is this seat taken?" Adam grinned down at her and pointed to the mostly empty pew.

Sara's heart took off like a sprinter at the starting gun. She slid down, making room for him at the aisle. "Hi. You came."

"Yep. You made it sound like something I needed to try." He sat beside her and tucked his Bible beside him. "How's your week been?"

"Busy. We're overbooked and understaffed. Patients are getting annoyed—which I can't blame them for—and that makes them even crankier than usual by the time they get to me."

"Are they usually cranky?"

"Often. Pain will do that." Sara shrugged. "Comes with the territory. Sometimes they remember we're trying to help. But the exercises hurt, too, so...How's your week been?"

"The word 'nightmare' comes to mind. But I did hear back from the mission downtown. Exciting stuff."

"Yeah?"

Adam opened his mouth but closed it as the pastor stood at the front of the room and clapped his hands for attention. "Let's open with prayer."

Sara tried to focus on the pastor's words. His prayers were always heartfelt and uplifting. Instructional, even. She'd frequently gone home and tried to write out her thoughts as prayers like Pastor Brown prayed. They never seemed as good, but God knew her heart.

Adam smelled nice. His cologne—deodorant?—was subtle and had hints of pine and sunshine. How did they make something smell like a sunny summer day and keep the pine from smelling antiseptic? Whatever they'd done, the result was worth it. And distracting.

He nudged her with his elbow and spread his Bible on his lap, shifting so she could share. Heat bloomed on her cheeks. She'd brought her own but...sharing with him was an excuse to move a little closer.

The pastor finished his short devotional and sat on the steps leading up to the platform. "Now, I'd like you to get in groups of two or three. Spend some time talking about what forgiveness means to you. You can be as vague or specific as you like—no need to get into the nitty-gritty with someone you don't know unless you want to. Then use your copy of this week's prayer list and spend the last ten minutes lifting up the needs of the congregation."

Sara cleared her throat. This was more than she'd anticipated. They'd been in small groups for prayer last week, too, and the pastor didn't usually do that two weeks in a row. "Um. We don't have to..."

"Don't be silly." He smiled and angled so their knees touched. "You want to go first?"

Sara shivered. She shook her head. "No, that's okay. You can."

Adam chuckled. "All right. Forgiveness. I guess to me it's always been what we have through Jesus and what we owe others. There's that bit in the Lord 's Prayer about forgiving us as we forgive those who have wronged us."

"Okay." That hadn't taken nearly as long as she'd needed to collect her thoughts. "Today seems to be throwing forgiveness at me from a lot of different angles. It came up at lunch. And then tonight. I spent my afternoon break looking up verses about forgiveness to help me wrestle with that lunch conversation. So, right now, when I think of forgiveness, I'm circling to Romans eight verse one. There is now no condemnation to those who are in Christ Jesus. That's the key there, isn't it? The end result of forgiveness?"

He nodded slowly.

What was he thinking? Sara cleared her throat. "So, if there's no condemnation, then we can't hold on to whatever it is either, can we?"

"Huh. I...would say no."

Sara nodded as her eyes started to burn. "It's hard, though. When you know there's so much that's been forgiven. Too much. Shouldn't there have to be some kind of penance?"

10

Unshed tears shone in Sara's eyes, and Adam's heart cracked. Even twenty minutes ago, he would have agreed with her that yes, there absolutely needed to be penance. Maybe not for a new believer, but certainly for someone who'd hit up the big sins while still claiming Jesus. Except the pastor had made a major deal out of the fact that God didn't see sins as big or little. One was just as bad as the next. He covered her hand with his and squeezed gently. "Molly said to me not too long ago that when we act that way, we're saying Jesus' death on the cross wasn't enough. That we somehow require more."

Sara blinked and a tear slipped down her cheek.

"It diminishes what He did for us. And we don't have the power to do that. Or the right to try." Adam swallowed. They weren't that different, he and Sara. They both thought they knew better than God when it came to dealing with sin. *Oh, Lord...forgive me.* "You want to pray?"

She took a deep breath and managed a weak smile. "Yeah. I didn't grab the prayer list—forgot. Did you get one?"

Adam slid a copy out of his Bible without letting go of her hand. He should let go, but he couldn't make his fingers release hers. She wasn't dragging her hand away, either. "Here. You want to open or close?"

"Close, I guess." Sara bowed her head and prayed for her heart to slow back to normal. Adam's voice was quiet, but still audible over the subtle murmur of voices that filled the sanctuary. His words were simple and earnest. Had she ever been that at home when she was praying?

When he stopped, she took a deep breath and offered a short prayer of her own. Her palms were sweating. It was never this hard to pray aloud when she was paired up with a random old lady.

"Amen." He squeezed her hand and released it.

"This is nice to see." Pastor Brown paused at their pew, his hand resting on Adam's shoulder. "You took my advice?"

Adam neck turned red as he nodded. "Yes, sir."

"Good. How are you, Sara?"

She smiled at the pastor. "Great, thanks. Busy, but that's life, right?"

The pastor laughed. "Indeed it is. Always nice to see you. Have a good night."

Sara watched the pastor move to the next group before looking at Adam. "Are you going to tell me what that's about?"

The flush on his cheeks deepened. "I'd rather not."

"Hmm." Should she let it go? His blush was kind of adorable. Wait. Adorable? That didn't matter. Wouldn't. There was nothing possible between them. Was there? No. He'd made it fairly clear there wasn't. "All right."

"Just like that?" He raised his eyebrows. "No girl lets someone off the hook that easily."

"Did you not want me to?"

"No, I did. I just didn't expect you to." Adam shrugged. "I appreciate it."

"You're welcome." Sara frowned. "To be clear, I'm not sure we know each other well enough to make sweeping generalizations about responses just yet."

"You're right. So...why don't we work on that?"

Her heart sped up. Was he saying...? "Work on what, exactly?"

"How well we know each other." His eyes locked with hers and he held her gaze. Her mouth went dry and the hum of conversation around them seemed to disappear. "Would that be okay?"

Sara nodded.

A slow smile spread over his face. "Great. Why don't we start with dinner? There's a great little deli not too far from here. I could drive and bring you back to your car when we're finished?"

She moistened her lips. "I'd like that."

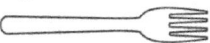

"Wednesday night is the new Friday, I take it?" Rebecca rocked the baby carrier on the floor by her chair and grinned at Sara. "I thought you hated him."

"I never said I hated him." Sara peeked at the sleeping infant and sighed. "How come she's never awake when I'm around? I want to hold her at some point."

"I'm sure she'll wake up before I go. When is Jen getting here?"

Sara shrugged. "She said she had to run a couple of errands on the way over. What else needs to happen for her wedding? I thought getting the dress handled finished up the list."

"Nope. Today is cake." Rebecca adjusted the blanket surrounding her daughter with a tiny smile.

"You're doting again." Sara chuckled. It was good to see. Not that anyone had ever doubted Rebecca would be an amazing mother—she'd always had that maternal urge. Unlike Sara. Sure, she wanted to hold the baby, but there was something comforting knowing she could give her back if there was an issue.

Rebecca laughed. "I can't even say I'm sorry."

"So absolutely no chance of you coming back to work?" The rest of the week had been as packed and horrible as the start. They'd interviewed two physical therapists, but Sara didn't hold out a lot of hope that either would be hired. She'd overheard a conversation when she'd been looking for a file in the records room that suggested they were considering keeping the practice at a lower staffing level to increase profits. If they did that...life wasn't going to get less stressful anytime soon.

"Maybe when she starts school. I'll keep current, but...it's so amazing to be home with her and get to experience everything first hand. Ben's a little jealous. I can see it sometimes when I'm telling him about our day—he gets a wistful look in his eye. But it's not like we can both stay home. Someone has to work. Still, he's going to look into working from home a day or two a week. He did that when he hurt his knee, so he's hopeful they'll let him."

At the knock on the door, Sara stood. "That's probably Jen."

Sara crossed the room and tugged open the door. Jen hurried in, shedding her coat and dropping her purse as she made her way to the couch.

"Hi. Sorry. The line at the pharmacy is crazy on Saturday, and they goofed up one of my meds, so they had to call the doctor—which is a feat on a weekend, as you can imagine and just ugh. And I didn't figure David was ready to face the madness of trying to navigate the medical nightmare of my life. Even though he did offer." Jen unwound a scarf from her neck and shrugged out of her coat before plopping into a chair at the table. "So what are we talking about and do you have any coffee?"

"Sara had another Wednesday date with Adam."

"It wasn't a date." Sara shook her head. "I'll get you coffee. Get Rebecca to tell you where we're looking at cakes. And why isn't David doing this with you again?"

"No way. I want to hear about the date first. And because he doesn't care about the cake. I have tried every way I can think of to get him to offer an opinion, and all he says is that he wants me to have what I want and as long as we get to go home together at the end of the night, he's happy."

Sara brought a mug of coffee and the carafe out to the table. She topped up her own cup and looked at Rebecca. "More?"

"Better not. I'm trying to keep the caffeine down to one cup a day since I'm nursing." She sighed. "I miss coffee."

Jen blew across the top of her drink before taking a long sip. "Ahh. Perfect. So let's hear about this date."

Sara groaned. "It. Wasn't. A. Date. We had dinner after prayer meeting."

"Again," Rebecca chimed in with a grin.

"Yes, fine, again. So what. We're getting to know each other. That's all." Sara didn't want to spill all the details of their conversation. Not just yet. It was still fresh and left her warm and tingly inside. Wasn't she allowed to have a secret or two? Jen and Rebecca certainly hadn't shared every single thing when they were in the process of falling in love. Falling in love? Not even on the table. Getting to know Adam wasn't the same thing as falling in love with him.

"Uh huh." Jen glanced at Rebecca. "Are we letting her dodge?"

"I guess for now. But only because we're due at the first bakery in about forty-five minutes, and it's going to take at least thirty of them to get over there." Rebecca stood and hauled the baby carrier up by its handle. "You know I have to drive, right? Because of the car seat?"

Jen nodded. "Shotgun."

"Darn it. You always do that." Sara drained her coffee and scowled at Jen. "Why haven't you grown out of high school yet?"

Jen beamed. "'Cause it works and has the side benefit of annoying you. Especially since you didn't want to talk about your evening with Adam."

"Look, it's not that I don't want to talk about it, it's just that there's nothing really to say. He's nice. Okay? I revoke my previous assessment of him. And yes, I think he's attractive. But that doesn't change anything. I'm not looking for romance. You two—of all people—should know I can't have that." Sara checked that the door to her apartment was locked and followed them to the elevator.

"Wait. Why can't you have romance?" Rebecca pushed the button and turned to frown at Sara.

"Because..."

"We just talked about this." Jen stepped into the elevator. "You've repented and been forgiven. Why are you still living like you're unworthy?"

"I'm not." Sarah pushed the button for the garage level. "But that doesn't mean I'm going to jump into a situation where I'm tempted to mess up all over again. Dating, falling in love, all of that? I...just don't think it's going to be for me. And I'm okay with that."

Rebecca and Jen exchanged a glance. Sara frowned. Fine. Let them. The smug married crowd—or nearly married, in Jen's case—comprised all of her friendships with the exception of Adam. If nothing else, spending time with him was refreshing simply because he didn't have that unquenchable glow that being in love gave people.

Sara stretched out on the couch and draped an arm over her eyes. She loved Jen and Rebecca like sisters, but shopping with them two weekends in a row was one weekend too many. Maybe both excursions had been relatively painless in the overall scheme of things. Successful, too. But...no more. She couldn't take any more.

She groaned when her phone rang. Why? Without looking at the caller ID, she answered. "Hello?"

"Sara? It's Adam...are you okay?"

Perfect. Why hadn't she checked the display? Then she could've answered with her cheerful, perky voice. "Hi. Yeah, I'm fine. Just ate way too much cake today."

"I'm sorry. I could swear you said 'too much cake,' but I'm not sure how those words go together."

Sara laughed. "Normally I would agree with you. But you—like me, prior to today—have clearly never been wedding cake shopping."

"Wedding...I thought...what?"

"Do you know Jen Andrews? She said she knew you a little." Sara winced. Way to go. Now he knew they'd talked about him. She should not talk on the phone when she was full of cake and exhausted. "She and David Pak are getting married on Valentine's Day. She hadn't chosen a cake yet."

"Oh. Right." His voice was considerably brighter. "And now she has?"

"Yes. Finally. But I'm still going to be so sick of cake that I won't enjoy it. A month isn't long enough to get over eating as much cake as we consumed today."

"That's too bad. I guess I'll let you go."

Seriously? "You don't have to do that. What's up?"

"Hmm? Oh, I was just calling to invite you to a cake eating party tonight." He started to snicker as he said the last words.

"You need to work on your delivery if you expect me to believe you." She smiled. It was still nice that he'd joke around. Like a friend would. A *platonic* friend. "Why'd you really call?"

There was a long stretch of silence. "Um. Oh. I didn't tell you I got in touch with the mission downtown, did I? That was a good call on your part. I spoke with my brothers after talking with them, and I think we're going to figure out how to work them into our schedule."

"Yeah? That's great. I know they need that space. I keep meaning to try and get down there—see if there's some way I can help out." Sara shifted on the couch. She'd meant to bring that up with Rebecca today, in fact. But between all the dessert sampling and baby care, plus intermittent attempts from both Rebecca and Jen to tease her about Adam, it had slipped her mind.

"So, thanks."

"You're welcome. I'm glad it worked out."

"Will I see you in Sunday school tomorrow?"

"Unless I die from cake exposure overnight, yes."

Adam laughed. "I'll save you a seat. 'Night."

"'Night." Sara smiled as she disconnected the call. Who would've ever thought that in just about a month she'd go from disliking Adam Lassiter to considering him one of her better friends?

11

"You've got it bad." Molly looked away from the game she was playing with Karl on the console in the living room.

Adam shook his head. "No, I don't."

"Right. Why'd you really call her? 'Cause I'm not buying the whole tell her about something you could've told her at church in the morning bit." Karl shook his head. "Frankly, I'm surprised she bought it."

"He has a point." Molly grinned.

"Why are you even here, Moll? Don't you usually have dates on Saturday nights?" Adam frowned. He should've made the call in his room. But he'd been planning to ask Sara out and, if she'd said yes, he would've been right by the door. Which was ridiculous. The apartment wasn't so big that it took more than seven extra seconds if he left from his room.

Molly and Karl exchanged a look. What was that about?

Karl cleared his throat. "This actually *is* a date."

"Oh, please. Try that on someone who doesn't know the two of you. Besides, not even you are lame enough to consider console gaming and ordered in pizza a date." Adam shook his head. Maybe he should call Sara back and suggest getting some ice cream.

Molly turned red stared at the TV.

"We're getting Chinese, actually. And since neither of us think it's lame, I guess maybe your opinion doesn't matter." Karl turned his attention back to the game.

Adam's jaw dropped. He was serious? Molly'd had a crush on his roommate for forever, but Karl actually clued in? That was impossible to wrap his mind around, despite the evidence in front of him. Molly. And Karl. Nope. It was a little too Twilight Zone.

Adam grabbed his keys from the bowl by the door and slipped out. He'd go...anywhere. Anywhere had to be better than here.

In his car, Adam kept on the back roads, wandering without a purpose in mind as he tried to process Karl dating Molly. Sure, they hung out together a lot—they were like the Three Musketeers. But he didn't remember reading the part where two of them fell in love with each other. Not that Molly and Karl were there yet. This had to be the first date, right? Karl had said he was getting ready to make a move.

Adam shuddered. Best not to think about that too hard.

What happened if it didn't work out? Seemed like no matter what, the three of them hanging out was no longer an option.

At a stoplight, he looked around, realized where he'd ended up, and laughed.

Fifteen minutes later, he took a deep breath and knocked on Sara's apartment door. Had she stayed in or had someone convinced her to go out? Would she even come to the door if she wasn't feeling great? Maybe he should've called. Except that had turned out so poorly the first time.

Locks snicked and the door opened a crack. "Adam?"

She really did look ill. Maybe this was a bad idea. He lifted the plastic sack from the grocery store and smiled. "I figured maybe you needed some ice cream to go with all that cake."

"I'm not sure 'need' and 'ice cream' ever go together but maybe it would soften up the solid mass of misfortune in my stomach. But I also don't think it's possible to feel worse. Come on in. What kind did you get?"

"Vanilla." He followed her into the apartment and looked around. It wasn't what he expected. The walls were bare, save for one lonely painting of enormous sunflowers over the fireplace. She had a small TV on top of a credenza along one wall and two loveseats forming an 'L' to give options to face it or the fireplace. One end table held a mismatched stack of books and some remotes. The only indication that she'd been in the room was an afghan draped over half of one loveseat spilling onto the floor.

"Who buys vanilla ice cream?" Sara planted her hands on her hips and scowled at him. "You're joking, right?"

"Um. No, actually. In my defense, I did also buy chocolate sauce, whipped cream, and maraschino cherries."

"Hm. You're forgiven. But I'm considering this an almost major black mark." Sara grinned. "Come on into the kitchen."

"I don't understand the general dislike of vanilla in the world." Adam set the grocery bag down on the kitchen table and tucked his hands in his pockets. "What's wrong with simple?"

"Nothing, I guess, when you put it that way. But how do you choose simple when there are flavors like moose tracks out there?" Sara got out two bowls from a cabinet and set them on the table before turning to rummage in a drawer.

Adam pulled out the contents of the bag one by one. "Is that your favorite?"

"No. It's just an example."

"So what is?"

Sara sat and pried open the ice cream. "I don't have one. I usually go with what strikes my fancy at the time."

"Ever go for vanilla?" Who didn't have a favorite flavor of ice cream? Adam sat opposite her and reached for the jar of cherries.

Sara frowned as she scooped the treat into her bowl. "Yeah, sometimes. The cones at the drive through...sometimes you need one."

Adam laughed. "So simple isn't always bad."

"I never said it was." She grinned. "But your point is noted. I retract my objection to your flavor selection."

"Thank you." He winked and squirted chocolate sauce over the top of the three scoops of vanilla in his bowl.

"What really brings you out this way?" Sara tapped the side of her dish with her spoon. "I know it wasn't just the ice cream."

A denial hovered on the tip of his tongue. Couldn't it be that simple? "Felt like getting out of the apartment...ended up here."

"Because...?"

His shoulders sank. What was he supposed to say? That he had a little crush on her and wanted to see if something could develop? There was no way that was the right approach. Things Sara had said the times they'd eaten together made it clear that she wasn't in the market for a relationship. "Molly is apparently dating my roommate, Karl."

Her eyebrows lifted. "That's new."

Adam nodded. "They're on their first date. On my couch."

Sara laughed. "No way."

Adam shrugged. "She didn't seem to mind."

"But you did."

It wasn't a question, but it was still ridiculous. "No. That's not it at all. I didn't want to be a third wheel. Who wants their friend horning in on a date?"

"Nobody."

He pointed his spoon at her. "Exactly. So I left and ended up here. Is that okay?"

There was the briefest hesitation before she nodded. "Of course. If you want to hang for a while, there's a new made for TV sci fi movie coming on in about a half hour. It's guaranteed to be horrible."

She watched those? That wasn't something he ever would've pegged. He grinned. "That's the best kind."

Karl was in his room when Adam got home. He hesitated by the door. Should he knock and ask how it had gone? Or was that prying? If the girl had been anyone other than Molly, he would've known what to do. But Molly was...Molly. What if was a disaster? Would that make things weird between the three of him? Was he going to get stuck in the middle?

Ugh.

Adam shook his head and continued down the hall. Tomorrow was soon enough to figure that out. Or maybe even the day after. There was no rush.

As he got ready for bed, he couldn't stop the smile that curved his lips. At least ice cream with Sara had gone well. The movie had been terrible, as promised, but she clearly loved it. Every time one of the slimy monsters had oozed out of the wall, she'd screamed and inched closer. They'd spent the last third of the movie with their legs and arms touching on one side. He'd been tempted to put his arm around her—more than tempted, if he was honest—but he'd managed to hold off. The wiser choice, certainly. He'd be her friend.

And then, when they were friends and she couldn't imagine life without him, that's when he'd ask her out.

12

"How'd you manage to snag Adam?"

Sara frowned at the girl—what was her name? They'd hung out a few times back when Sara had been more interested in finding dates than listening to the lessons at church. Jessica, maybe? "We're friends, that's all."

"Oh, sure." Jessica rolled her eyes. "I know you. All of us do."

"I'm not like that anymore." Sara's heart drummed a rapid tattoo in her chest. "Maybe you shouldn't be either."

"Puh-lease. When you're done with him, let him know I'm interested." She offered a shark-tooth smile. "I figured he'd be stuck with the goody two shoes for life. I seriously need to know your technique. There are a handful of other guys I wouldn't mind seeing migrate to the dark side."

Sara swallowed the bile that had crawled up her throat as the girl flounced off. She needed to warn Adam off. He deserved better than getting lumped into that camp. He deserved better than someone like her.

"Hey."

Sara turned and smiled in spite of herself. "Hi. Look, Adam, you shouldn't sit with me today."

He drew his eyebrows together. "Why not?"

"Because people are starting to talk. They think you and I are together." Heat burned across her cheeks as she saw Jessica glancing in their direction.

"Would that be so bad?"

She blinked. "No. But you don't need your reputation dragged through the muck. Just..."

He held up a finger. "I'm not worried about it. You shouldn't be either."

But she was. "I really don't think you should do this."

"Do you want me to sit with you?" His gaze locked with hers and she found herself swimming in the deep blue of his eyes.

She nodded.

He grinned. "Okay then, let's sit."

She let him take her elbow and steer her toward the back row. Her pulse quickened and she forced herself not to meet anyone's eyes. Were they all thinking along the same lines as Jessica? Sara slid down in her seat. This was a bad idea.

"Hi, there." Molly dropped into the chair on Sara's other side with a huge smile. "You don't mind if Karl and I sit with you two, do you?"

Before Sara could answer, Adam leaned forward and shook his head. "Of course not. How was last night?"

"Good." Molly cocked her head to one side. "You didn't have to leave, you know."

"Yes. I did. Nobody wants their roommate—or their friend—hanging out during their date. And no friend-slash-roommate wants to do that, either." Adam made a show of shuddering.

Molly laughed. "What'd you end up doing?"

Adam glanced at Sara, an eyebrow quirked up.

Sara swallowed. Was he asking her permission? She wanted to shake her head. Or make some witty comment that made it seem like she didn't know. Instead, she gave a slight nod. At least Molly and Karl would know the truth when whatever story Jessica spun started making the rounds.

"Grabbed some ice cream and caught Octozilla on TV."

Molly's eyebrows drifted up and her gaze latched onto Sara. "There's no way you watch monster movies."

Sara hunched her shoulders. "They're a guilty pleasure."

"You're not serious." Molly stared at her. "You're shattering all my preconceived notions."

"Sorry about that." Sara shook her head. Why did people find that so surprising?

"No you aren't." Molly patted Sara's arm. "And you shouldn't be, either. I'm sorry for assuming things about you."

Sara shrugged. "Seems to be what everyone likes to do."

Adam winced and took her hand in his. He squeezed gently. "Don't worry about them, okay?"

Sara didn't miss Jessica's intent scrutiny of the situation and tugged her hand free. "You don't know what you're saying. But it's a nice thought."

"I..." Adam trailed off as the teacher moved to the front of the class and called everyone to order. "We're not done with this conversation."

Sara smiled. He could think that, if he wanted. But she wasn't going to drag him down. He deserved better. And if he couldn't see it, well, she'd just have to do it for him.

"Hey. What are you doing downtown?" Rebecca looked up from the book she was peering at.

Sara shrugged. She wasn't actually sure. But after spending most of the week in her apartment trying to avoid Adam, the walls were starting to close in on her. "Just needed to get out. You and Ben always have such great things to say about the homeless mission, I figured I'd see what I could do to help."

"Yeah? What'd Jerry say?" Rebecca pointed to a spot on the page and turned to the teen beside her. "I think you'll find the answer in here."

"To come down and take a look around and he'd come find me when he had a minute and we could talk about possibilities." Sara glanced at the table where several teens were doing schoolwork. "I'm not sure tutoring is going to be my thing though."

Rebecca chuckled. "That's okay. You know, I keep meaning to ask Jerry about doing a walk-in clinic of sorts for PT. Maybe that's something the three of us could discuss. There are a lot of homeless who end up with injuries that never get fully healed. If we provided some exercises, maybe a few supportive wraps when warranted, it might help relieve pain, at least."

"It's a good idea. Not really a solution, but...is it better than nothing?" That was a lot like what she'd done in Jamaica. Sara blew out a breath. Was it better than nothing? Or did it have the potential to cause harm? Even though Adam had apologized—and they'd been on their way to being friends—the concern was something to consider. "You don't think it could hurt?"

Rebecca frowned. "I don't see how stretching or doing the same simple exercises we send people home with instructions to do every day unsupervised between appointments can be a problem. What's going on?"

"I don't know." Sara pulled out a chair and sat. "And this probably isn't the place to worry about it. You're supposed to be helping."

"They know they can interrupt when they need to, right, D'Andre?"

The boy sitting next to Rebecca grinned. "Yep." He turned his attention to Sara. "You any good at algebra?"

"A little. Maybe. Why?"

"'Cause Miss Rebecca can't figure this out, and neither can the rest of us." He slid a sheet of paper across the table.

Sara glanced down at it and laughed. She turned to Rebecca. "Does Zach know you help his students?"

"He knows I try. But he can also usually tell when I've been involved, because the answers are wrong." Rebecca shrugged. "Everyone has their strengths."

"True." Sara looked down at the paper again and spotted the error the boy—D'Andre?—had made. She made a little mark in the margin next to the line that had the problem. "Double check here. I think you're on the right track, but you've got an error that's throwing you off."

D'Andre took the paper. Lips moving silently, he moved his finger across the numbers before muttering, "Aw, shi-oot."

Sara covered her laugh with a cough.

Rebecca shook her head. "Nice catch. Almost."

"Sorry." D'Andre's shoulders jerked up. "It's hard to stop."

"There you are. Sorry to keep you waiting." Jerry strolled up to the table and grinned. "Why don't you come on back to my office and we'll see where to plug you in."

Sara stood. "Bye. Nice to meet you, D'Andre."

The kid raised a finger, his focus intent on the math paper in front of him.

"I'll call you later and you can tell me what Jerry says. And what's going on with you and Adam." Rebecca wiggled her eyebrows.

Sara sighed. Maybe talking it over with Rebecca would help.

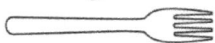

On Sunday morning, Sara sat on the couch with her Bible open on her lap. Talking with Rebecca—and then the rest of the gang, since she'd let herself get dragged into dinner at Season's Bounty after leaving the homeless mission downtown—hadn't helped. No one, absolutely no one, understood the problem. It all boiled down to Adam being a grownup who was capable of making his own decisions. Which of course he was. But he didn't understand just how bad it was going to get if they actually started dating.

Which was also a bit of an assumption.

It wasn't as if he'd asked her out. But the ice cream and the flirty texts, not to mention that he went out of his way to touch her hand or her arm...those were indications he was interested.

She was interested, too.

Sara buried her face in her hands. What was she supposed to do? She believed with her whole heart that her sins were forgiven. But the singles class wasn't likely to let her forget and move on. Take Jessica. She'd spent the whole class last week shooting looks in Sara's direction. After class, she'd tried to corner Adam. Thankfully, Molly and Karl had called him away. And Jessica was just one—but it felt like so many followed her lead. Sara had tried to separate herself from that group—had mostly succeeded—and it clearly upset them.

And when that group was upset, they could be vicious.

Thus, church at home. Because, whether or not he realized it, Adam needed a week where he wasn't seen with Sara.

She ignored the little clutch in her heart. She missed him. Ridiculous, but true. She focused her attention on the words of Romans eight and reminded herself, for the fiftieth time today, that Adam was better off without her.

13

This was ridiculous. Yesterday was the third Sunday in a row that Sara hadn't come to church. Or at least to Sunday school. He hadn't seen her in the service, but there were four other options to choose from—one of which was on Saturday night—so it was entirely possible she'd simply made a change. But why?

She hadn't been coming to Wednesday night prayer meeting either. That was a bigger concern. She'd loved it—and he understood exactly why. He'd been attending faithfully for the last month, and even though she wasn't there, it never failed to be just the thing he needed mid-week. Except he'd rather share it with Sara.

She hadn't cut him off completely. She'd return a text, maybe two, every week. But not right away. Sometimes two days would pass before she replied. It was time to stop the madness.

Adam checked the time on the dash of his truck. Perfect. He sent up a quick prayer for the right words and pushed open the door. The parking lot of the strip mall that lined the road in front of the block of medical offices was packed with lunchtime traffic. Clumps of people strolled down the sidewalk, their laughter floating on the icy breeze. February wasn't in a hurry to turn mild, it seemed.

He pulled open the door of the sub shop and smiled as he spotted Sara. She was seated at the back table, a sandwich and book on the table in front of her.

"Is this seat taken?"

Sara looked up. Her eyes lit for just a moment before her expression turned to one of confusion. "Well, kinda. I'm expecting Jen and maybe Rebecca...why are you here, Adam?"

He pulled out the chair and sat, crossing his arms on the table as he leaned forward and held her gaze. "Because I miss you."

Her mouth opened and she took a breath before letting it out and shaking her head.

"I thought we agreed you'd let me worry about my reputation?"

"We never agreed. You said it didn't matter. But Adam, it does. You don't know these people like I do. And you deserve better than that." Her gaze drifted over his shoulder.

"You can stop watching the door, they aren't coming."

Sara furrowed her brow. "What do you mean? Jen confirmed the time by text this morning."

"Because I asked her to make sure you'd be here. I wanted to see you—to talk to you." He paused and cleared his throat, gathering his thoughts and praying for the right words. "I realize we've only really known each other a month. And okay, we didn't start out on the best foot. But after that...I consider you a friend. A good one. And I'm not willing to lose that just because some people may or may not have an issue with that."

"A friend." Sara tucked a piece of hair behind her ear.

"To start, yeah."

"To st—what do you mean?"

This was it. His heart pounded in his chest and he swallowed. "I like you. You're smart and funny...and beautiful."

"No...Adam, I can't—"

"Hear me out. I'm not saying we're going to get married or anything, but I wouldn't rule it out, down the road. But first, maybe we could go out to dinner. On purpose."

"Like a date?"

"Like a date." He grinned. She hadn't gotten up and stormed out of the restaurant, so he was going to call it a win. Or at least a partial one.

"Are you sure? You know about me...I'm not the kind of person you've been saving yourself for. And Jessica—at church?—she's going to assume all kind of things and take great joy in spreading it around."

He shrugged.

"Adam..."

"I'm not blowing you off, I promise. But the people in that group already say things about me that aren't true. The last one I heard had me scared of girls and committed to a single life. None of which is true."

"Okay, but that's harmless."

"So is whatever else they come up with, because I know the truth, and more importantly, so does God."

"I guess."

"So is that a yes?" It wasn't the most enthusiastic response, but if it meant she'd stop avoiding him—and that they could do something more officially date-like, he'd take it.

"Yeah." She pressed her lips together. "I can't help thinking this is a mistake, though."

He grinned and reached for her hand. "Your objection is noted. If I go get a sandwich are you going to run off?"

Sara checked the time on her phone. "I still have twenty minutes on my lunch break."

"All right. Then when I get back, let's talk about what you'd like to do on Friday night." Adam barely resisted the urge to pump his fist in the air. For the first time in a long while, he was ready for the week to go by fast.

"Did she say anything about why she'd been skipping?" Molly got a glass down from the cabinet and filled it at the sink.

Adam leaned against the counter and shook his head. It was weird having Molly here for a date with Karl. She was used to running tame in their apartment—it wasn't that. But knowing she was only hanging out with him because Karl was late was odd. Not bad. Just...different. "More of the same. Trying to save my reputation. And she'd been going on Saturday night, so that's at least something."

Molly snickered. "Your reputation could use a little tarnishing. You practically have a halo."

"Whatever."

"It's true. When was the last time you dated someone?"

Adam lifted a shoulder. The honest truth was that he hadn't seen the point. Once he'd realized he and Molly weren't going to get together, there wasn't anyone who interested him. He kept waiting and praying for God to make it clear who He had in mind and there was nothing. Until Sara. And okay, sure, that hadn't seemed ideal at first, but the more he got to know her, the more possible it seemed.

"Please tell me it wasn't when we went out."

Adam shrugged again.

"That was two years ago!" Molly shook her head. "If I'd known that I would've pushed harder with the dates I tried to set up for you."

"Well, I'm glad you didn't know, then. It's fine. I don't feel like I missed anything. Besides, before Karl, how long ago was your last date?"

Molly's cheeks turned a deep scarlet. "We aren't talking about me."

"Uh huh." Adam pointed his finger at her. "Pot."

She pointed back with a grin. "Kettle. Fine. But you weren't even interested. You know I've had my eye on Karl for a while."

"True." And he'd wondered if his roommate was ever going to clue in. So now that he had, why was Adam so uncomfortable? "I'm happy for you."

Molly raised an eyebrow.

"I am. It's just a little weird. I'll get over it."

"You'd better. Maybe having your own girlfriend will help."

Girlfriend? He hadn't thought of Sara in those terms. They were friends, certainly. And they'd be going out on a date on Friday. But girlfriend? That seemed like jumping the gun just a little. He wasn't opposed. At all. But she might be.

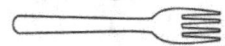

Adam forced his hands to unclench and took a deep breath. He'd eaten with Sara before. This was the same. Just because they were calling it a date didn't change the fundamental premise. They'd sit down, eat, and talk. There was no reason for the herd of stampeding buffalo currently pretending his stomach was the wide-open plains.

Sara opened her apartment door with a smile. "Almost ready. You want to come in?"

"Sure." He followed and tried not to stare. She'd dressed up—at least, he'd never seen her in a skirt before. Not even at church. Of course, not many people wore nice clothes to church. It was casual and everyone seemed to have embraced that. He cleared his throat. "You look nice."

"Thanks. Go ahead and sit, I just need maybe three minutes." She disappeared down the hall.

What did she need to do? She looked...amazing. And he'd said nice. Adam cringed. Great way to start the date. He needed to step up his game.

"Okay, ready." Sara had a little purse in her hands and had put on knee-length boots that did amazing things to her legs. An image of her legs at the beach in Jamaica flashed through his mind and he quickly squashed it. That was definitely not the way to get things off on the right foot.

"Great. You never did say where you wanted to eat, so I chose a little Mexican place in Shirlington. Is that okay?" It wasn't like they had a reservation, so if she didn't want to go there, it was easy to change.

"Sure. Let me grab my coat. It's icy out there today. I keep hoping we'll get some snow, and then nothing."

Adam laughed and held the door for her as they left her apartment. "I'm grateful, to be honest. We're doing inside work on all the projects I'm heading up, but snow always throws a wrench in the schedule, if only because the traffic gets even worse."

"That's true. I don't like driving in the stuff if I can avoid it." She smiled and slipped her hand into his as the elevator doors slid open.

"Doesn't look like it's going to be an issue this year, at any rate." He squeezed her fingers, reveling in their warmth. "Anything fun at work this week?"

Sara laughed. "Nothing out of the ordinary. What about you?"

The elevator reached the lobby and they stepped out, walking through the small foyer to the parking lot where his truck was parked in one of the visitor spots. Adam opened her door before hurrying around to his side. The wind was like needles of ice that blew straight through his jacket.

"Brr."

Sara chuckled. "You can say that again. So, Shirlington? I don't get up there that often."

Adam shrugged. "I'm not there a ton myself, but I've always liked it."

Silence filled the cab of the truck, save for the radio playing the local Christian station. He didn't always listen to them—he didn't have a problem with most secular music—but there were times when having that quiet reminder of God's love was calming. Before long, they were on the highway headed toward the little spot of suburban nightlife. He cleared his throat. "So, I've been working with Jerry up at the mission in D.C.?"

"Yeah? How's that going?"

"He has big dreams and slowly but surely, they're making them reality. It's hard this time of year when it gets so cold, the number of homeless seeking shelter more than triples, and they do their best to fit in as many as they can. The new building will be a big help next year."

"They can't use it now?"

Adam shook his head. "I wish. But the reason they were able to purchase it as cheaply as they did is that it's been condemned. And

Jerry's worried that some of the folks who used to squat in there on the colder nights are going to end up hurt because, in his efforts to help them, they've temporarily lost their shelter."

"That's tough."

"Tell me. I had an idea, but...I don't know anyone who lives down there. Do you?"

Sara's eyebrows lifted. "Yeah. Zach and Amy—two of the group of friends I inherited when Rebecca and Ben got together—they're actually not far from the mission. And Amy's parents are pretty close, too. Why?"

"Do they go to church downtown, too?"

Sara nodded.

"I was thinking maybe some of the churches could open their classroom spaces or fellowship halls, like they would in an emergency."

"Wouldn't that open the church up to the possibility of theft?"

"Maybe. But I wondered if Jerry might have enough resources to staff the spaces, even if it was sparse. He might not. But I didn't want to bring it up to him until I had a direction to point him. I get the feeling he has so many balls in the air that throwing a new idea at him is only going to disrupt his ability to handle what he has going, unless there's a plan or sorts attached to the idea."

Sara smiled. "That makes sense. If you want, I can talk to Zach and see what he thinks?"

"Sure. You can give him my number if he has questions."

"I'll do that."

Adam exited the highway and in minutes, they were searching the rows of a parking garage for a spot. "It's crowded."

"Friday night." Sara laughed. "I take it that's not the day you usually get down here?"

"Nope. I like Tuesdays. It's never crowded on a Tuesday. Oh, hey, there's one." He cranked the wheel and slid the truck into the narrow spot. "You have enough room to get out over there?"

Sara leaned over to look out the window. "Should be okay."

He shifted into park and cut the engine. "All right, then. Shall we?"

14

Sara hovered at the intersection of the hallways that led to the singles group. She didn't want to miss Adam, but she had no interest in going to class. Adam might say he didn't care what people said about them being a couple, but she wasn't going to put that to the test if she didn't have to.

Molly breezed by then stopped and retraced her steps. "Hey. Coming to class?"

"Trying not to. I was going to see if I could grab Adam and maybe talk him into a different one."

Molly offered a sympathetic smile. "I think he's already in there. Want me to go look and send him out?"

"Would you?"

"Sure. I'll either be out in a minute, or he will."

Sara watched Molly stride off and leaned against the wall, waving absentmindedly to a woman who smiled at her as she walked by. Was she worrying too much? She wanted...something...with Adam. She hadn't pinned down exactly what, but he was different. Special. She *liked* him. As a person, not just as a handsome man. It was the first time friendship had played a factor in a relationship since, what, college?

"Hey. Aren't you coming in?" Adam reached for her hand as he closed the distance between them in the rapidly clearing hall. "I think they'll be starting soon."

"I was wondering if we could try a different group." She shifted, her belly jittering.

Adam studied her for a long minute before nodding slowly. "If it would make you happier, I guess. I still think you're giving them too much hold over your life."

"Maybe I am, but I'm not sure you understand how vicious they can be. If I can save you even a little bit of that, I want to."

He smiled. "Let me go grab my Bible and then we can find another class."

"I had one in mind—the McGregors are leading it."

"Who...oh, the pastor's daughter and her husband?"

Sara nodded. She didn't know Lydia super well, but the few conversations she'd had at various women's events had impressed her. Lydia knew what it was like to fall from grace and find a way back to God. Her story was incredible, and she wasn't shy about sharing it. Maybe one day Sara would get to that point as well. For now, it seemed like a reasonable class to try, even if most of the folks who attended were married couples.

Adam hurried back down the hall, his Bible under his arm. "Okay, lead on."

"Thanks for doing this."

"It's no big deal. Honestly, I think about trying something new every month or so. After two or three years out of college, the singles class doesn't feel like it fits anymore."

"So why do you stay?" Sara studied the room numbers and tried to remember which way they needed to go.

"Habit, mostly. And I have friends there—Molly and Karl at the top of the list. Now you."

She smiled, heat warming her cheeks. "Okay...I think this is it."

"Great." He reached for the knob.

"Before we go in...are you busy Wednesday?" Sara's heart hammered in her chest. Was she really going to ask him out rather than waiting for him to bring up a second date?

"Just a usual day at work, then prayer meeting. I was hoping I'd see you there this week. Why?"

"Would you go to Jen and David's wedding with me, instead?"

"On Wednesday. Who gets married on a Wednesday?"

Now it was awkward. He obviously hadn't been paying attention to the calendar. Why would he, though? They were too new of a couple. Were they even a couple? Friends who'd been on a date didn't necessarily translate into a couple. Did it? She cleared her throat. "People who want to get married on Valentine's Day?"

"Valen..." His face turned bright pink. It was kind of adorable. "Right. That's Wednesday."

She nodded. "So...the wedding? If you didn't have plans?"

His gaze met hers, his blue eyes working their calming magic. "The only person I'd want to have plans with is standing in front of me. I'd love to go to the wedding with you."

It was like a weight had lifted off her shoulders. "Yay!"

He chuckled. "Now are you ready to try this class?"

"Absolutely."

"Why am I so nervous?" Jen paced the length of the small classroom they'd used for the bride's room and wrung her hands together. "I'm marrying the most amazing man. I shouldn't be nervous."

"Don't look at me. I've never even been engaged." Sara ran a hand down the skirt of her cranberry red bridesmaid dress. "But I do appreciate you letting me wear the dress from Rebecca's wedding. I love this thing."

"It looks amazing on you and it fit the color scheme. And Rebecca fits in mine, since she hasn't lost all her baby weight yet, so everybody wins." Jen shook her hands and breathed out. "Why isn't she here yet?"

"She's picking up the flowers on her way. I'm sure she'll drop the boutonnieres off with the guys before heading back here. And in between, I'm guessing she'll have to check in with Ben to make sure the baby's happy."

"You're right. I'm obsessing. Sorry."

Sara shrugged. "I think you're allowed on your wedding day. Did you remember to eat lunch?"

Jen nodded. "Yes, Mom."

"Speaking of mom, where's yours? I figured she'd be in here making us all crazy."

"I made Dad promise to keep her busy until right before hand. She can't even talk about the wedding without sobbing—good tears, but still. I didn't want to wreck my makeup since I'm bothering to wear it."

There was a knock on the door a second before Rebecca hurried in carrying a big box. "Hi. Sorry. I wanted to check on the baby real quick."

Sara pointed at Jen. "See?"

"I'm predictable. I know this." Rebecca shook her head. "And I feel like I should apologize for making you two wear this dress. It's itchy."

"Mine isn't. Do you still have the tag in it?" Sara crooked a finger at Rebecca.

"No. It's probably just me. Anyway, I saw Adam out in the foyer." Rebecca wiggled her eyebrows. "He's looking mighty fine. And he brought you flowers."

Heat washed through Sara. "Really? That's..."

"Sweet. The word you're looking for is sweet." Jen grinned. "Speaking of flowers?"

"Oh, right." Rebecca set the box down and pulled out two small white boxes. She set those aside before lifting out a larger one. "This thing is amazing."

Jen reached for the box and flipped off the lid. "Ohhhh. It really is."

"Well, take it out so we can all see it." Sara tapped her foot.

Chuckling, Jen lifted out the waterfall bouquet of red roses. Tiny dots of baby's breath puffed up between the roses, adding texture and a hint of white. She held the flowers at her waist. "What do you think?"

"Gorgeous." Sara's eyes filled and she blinked back the tears. Both of her best friends were going to be married and then what?

Rebecca already had less time for them, as did most of the rest of the gang. It was the end of an era...and she wasn't ready for it. She cleared her throat and reached for the smaller boxes. "I want to see mine."

"Me, too." Rebecca took one and opened it.

Sara smiled at the miniature version—minus the waterfall—of Jen's bouquet. "Lovely. Thank you."

"I didn't see why I should be the only one with pretty flowers." Jen crossed the room and slung an arm over each of their shoulders. "I hope you know how much I love you two. This whole thing with David...it never would've happened without you."

Rebecca laughed. "Since you met him at my wedding, I guess that's true. But I'm awfully glad it did."

Sara gave her friend a one-armed hug before glancing at the clock on the wall. It was ten until four. "Shouldn't your mom be here by now? They're starting seating right at four, aren't they?"

Jen nodded.

"Want me to go find her?" Sara set her flowers down.

"Yeah...would you? We have to be completely out of here by six since there are activities tonight. Even though we're just using the side chapel, I don't want to get off schedule."

"You got it." Sara crossed to the door and reached for the doorknob just as it opened. She laughed. "I was just coming to find you."

Jen's mother swept into the room, beaming. "You all look lovely. Especially you, Jennifer."

"Thanks, Mom." Jen wrapped her arms around her mom. "I'm really doing this."

"Of course you are." Her mother leaned back and studied her face. "David is the perfect man for you. He understands you better than anyone I know, including your father and me. It won't always be easy. No marriage is. But I believe the two of you are committed to God and to one another and you're going to do the work that it takes to make things last."

Jen nodded.

Sara turned back to her flowers and picked them up. Work. Of course, marriage was work. She knew that—in her head at least. If marriage was work, it made sense that the relationship leading up to that would be as well. No one she'd dated before had been worth the kind of effort she associated with work. But Adam? She could see herself working to keep him.

"Earth to Sara." Rebecca poked Sara in the ribs.

"Hey." Sara squirmed away. "What?"

"You ready?"

Sara looked at Rebecca and then at Jen and nodded. "Let's do this."

15

Adam laid his hand on Sara's shoulder. "Is this seat taken?"

"There you are." She grinned and moved her bouquet from the place setting. "I'm sorry I couldn't ride over with you. With the pictures and then making sure we got everything cleaned up, I didn't think you'd want to hang out that long. Not when you could be here sampling whatever treats they have on those circulating trays. I looked for you when we got here. Where were you hiding?"

"Some of the guys—Zach and, um, Jack or Jackson, something like that, and...one other guy, I've forgotten his name—found a little lounge that had the TV on. Basketball. But I think it must've been a replay. I can't think why there'd be an actual game on a Wednesday evening." Adam shrugged. "Still, it beat milling around looking for someone I knew."

Sara laughed. "Ben, probably. That's the male half of the gang. Though I don't understand why Paige and Amy weren't with them."

"Maybe they were. There were girls. Women." His cheeks burned. It was always supposed to be women, not girls. But he had a hard time keeping that in mind—guys and girls was too ingrained. Thankfully, he hadn't run into anyone who got really bent out of shape about it. Well, Molly did sometimes, but that was mostly to give him a hard time. Probably. "Anyway. How were the pictures?"

Sara shrugged. "Lots of smiling. The more weddings I'm in, the more I think I want to do the pictures before the ceremony and not keep everyone waiting. These were fast and they still took, what, almost an hour?"

"About that. You're not worried about the groom seeing you beforehand?"

"Are you?"

Adam blinked.

Red flooded her face. "Not that—I don't mean—it's just luck, right? Do you worry about luck? I have Jesus. I don't need luck."

He nodded. "Okay. I can see that. I...never really thought about it, to be honest, or about what's behind the tradition."

"Why would you?" She glanced around the rapidly filling room. "I don't think I would have ever thought of looking at neighborhood clubhouses for a reception, either. Jen's folks live here though, so they got a great deal. Beats trying to find a hotel space or restaurant, though Jen was disappointed they couldn't do it at church. Valentine's Day being a Wednesday threw a wrench in their plans."

He chuckled, though he didn't see the big deal about the fourteenth of February. It had always been just another day...he certainly wouldn't want to memorialize it with something as meaningful as a wedding anniversary. Took all kinds, though. "Did I mention how nice you look?"

Sara beamed at him. "You didn't. Thank you. I could say the same."

Adam ran a hand down his tie. "I wasn't sure about the whole suit thing, but I'm glad I'm not overdressed. My brothers had fun ribbing me about the tie."

"You wore that to work?"

"No. I took the suit along in my truck, though. I knew I wouldn't have time to get home to change. So I got ready at the last job site, which happened to be where I met up with my brothers for a quick conversation about a couple of projects. Including the mission."

"Yeah?"

Adam nodded. "Jerry's contacting some of the nearby churches, as well as the elementary school where Zach teaches. He said they were making some headway and at least had emergency shelter in place, which is good. That building really isn't safe, so we want to get in and start demo as soon as we can."

"Are you going to have to knock the whole thing down?"

"Oh, no. The outside structure is pretty solid. There might be a little foundation work to do—need to evaluate that more closely. But inside...it's a mess. The stairs are just waiting to fall. Stuff like that."

"Ladies and gentlemen, if I can have your attention please." The DJ's microphone was loud. Conversation around them quieted quickly. "I'd like to introduce for the first time, Mr. and Mrs. David Pak."

Sara clapped as Jen and David walked into the room holding hands and beaming at one another. Adam's heart gave a little clutch and he glanced over at her. It didn't take much imagination to see her dressed in white, smiling up at him like Jen was doing to David right now. He swallowed and shot up a prayer for continued guidance. Now that God seemed to be pointing him to the mission field right here in his backyard...was Sara the next step? Was she the wife his heart ached for?

"How was the wedding?" Karl was sprawled across the couch, e-reader in hand. He hit the button on the bottom of his device and set it aside.

"Nice. Very Valentine's Day."

Karl snorted. "What's that mean?"

"Red and white everywhere. And hearts. Lots of hearts."

"So...tacky."

"No. No, it wasn't tacky. There was just no way you could forget that it was Valentine's Day." Adam shrugged out of his suit jacket and hung it over the back of kitchen chair. "I can't explain it better than that."

"Doesn't matter. Mostly curious. And Sara?"

Adam looked at his roommate. What was he getting at? "She's doing fine."

"And?"

"And what?" Adam rooted through a cabinet in the kitchen, finally emerging with a box of cookies. He set them on the table before filling a glass with milk and sitting down. He dunked the chocolate, cream-filled treat in his milk before stuffing it into his mouth.

Karl wiggled up on the couch and shook his head. "How are things?"

"Good, I think. Look, we went out Friday. We hung out at church and for lunch Sunday. We're texting a lot during the day when we have a chance, and she asked me to come to the wedding. I like her. A lot. But we've been friends what, six weeks now? It's a little early to declare my undying love and ask her to be my bride." Adam tried to keep a slightly snarky tone as he spoke, because the honest truth was that he wasn't convinced that it was too soon. But the signals Sara gave off suggested that, at least for her, it was. Love was a big deal. And even if he didn't have previous experience with the emotion to base anything on, he was pretty sure he'd tiptoed right into it when he wasn't looking.

Karl grunted.

"What's that mean?"

"Just find it interesting that undying love is on your mind, that's all."

Adam took another cookie and dunked it. "What about you and Molly? You know I'm going to have to kick your butt if you hurt her, right?"

"Goes without saying." Karl scratched his chin. "Why didn't you tell me she had a crush on me?"

Adam raised his eyebrows. "Seriously? Are we girls?"

"I'm just saying, a heads up would've been nice. I never would've bothered with Jessica. And honestly, I kind of feel like you owe me for that."

"How? How can I possibly be responsible for your previous bad taste in women? It's not like you didn't know Molly. She was over here almost as much as she is now. It's not my problem you couldn't see what was right under your nose."

Karl sighed. "I guess. She's great though, isn't she?"

"I've always thought so."

"Wait." Karl sat up, his feet hitting the floor with a *thunk*. "You don't have a thing for her, do you?"

"Molly?" Adam shook his head. "I wanted to, but we both agreed that we're better off as friends. The field's clear there, man."

"Okay. That's good." Karl blew out a breath. "It's weird to be so...possessive, I guess. It's never been a problem."

"Yeah, well, you haven't exactly dated quality women in the past."

"Yeah, yeah. At least I date. When was the last time you had a girlfriend again? High school?"

College. And Karl knew it. But there was no point in arguing. The general idea was the same. Adam hadn't done a lot of dating since he left school, it was true. "I still don't see the point in dating someone there's no chance of a future with. Can you honestly say you would've considered marrying Jessica? Or any of the women before her?"

Karl winced.

"Exactly." Adam dug out another cookie. "Speaking of Jessica."

"That's never a good way to open a sentence."

Adam grinned. "She's not that bad, is she?"

"You're kidding, right? When I told her I didn't think we should see each other anymore she," Karl made air quotes, "accidentally forwarded the consolatory email wherein her friend agreed that I was probably questioning my sexual preferences to the entire Sunday school class. You don't remember that?"

"Nope. I don't tend to open email that's from the group list though. It's never anything useful. If you pay attention during announcements or read the bulletin, you know everything that's going on."

"You're a very small minority." Karl rubbed the back of his neck. "I'm not completely sure that whole thing is blown over. With Jessica, you just never know."

Adam winced. So maybe Sara was right and the woman was a beast, that didn't mean he was going to live his life in fear of her. Although, wasn't that just what they were doing by trying different small groups rather than going to the singles class as a couple?

"Why?"

"Sara's worried. I guess Jessica said something that made Sara think my reputation was at stake if we got together." Adam shrugged. "I'm not really worried about it, but she keeps bringing it up."

"I wouldn't put it past her, honestly. Do you care?"

That was the real question. Adam shook his head. "Not really. It's not like I have a ton of friends in that class. There's you and Molly, now Sara and her friends."

"They've mostly left, haven't they?"

"Yeah."

"So it's probably fine." Karl reached for his e-reader. "Don't eat all the cookies."

Adam closed up the container and patted it before draining his milk. He wasn't going to worry about it. It was like he'd told Sara...they couldn't do anything major. Even if Jessica wanted to spread rumors. So what? He'd know the truth. So would Sara. So would any real friends. And most importantly, so would God.

No, Jessica's potential plotting wasn't anything to spend another minute on. How he felt about Sara though? His lips curved. He could spend quite a while longer thinking about that.

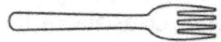

Adam parked his truck on the street in front of the D.C. mission's new building. This project had his juices flowing more than anything he'd been part of in a long time. Well, except for the buildings in Jamaica. There again he'd felt that same stirring—like what he did mattered. It wasn't that building—of fixing—someone's home didn't matter. It did. But it wasn't the same as doing something he *knew* helped.

He grabbed the tube holding the final plans that he'd picked up from their architect on the way over. Hopefully, Jerry would be pleased and the project could get underway.

Pulling open the front door, he smiled. The shelter was always busy, and the quiet hum of conversation was homey. There were classes going on in the rooms he passed—two of them looked like they were cooking related, the other could be anything. He hadn't gotten a glimpse of the whiteboard he knew stretched across one wall. Jerry said they tried to offer life-skills primarily; things that would help the men find jobs and make a way to stay off the streets.

At Jerry's office, Adam paused and knocked.

"Come in."

Adam pushed the door open and smiled. "Hi, Jerry. I brought the plans."

"You did? That's excellent." Jerry looked at his overflowing desk and frowned. "You know what? Let's go in the common room. The kids aren't out of school yet, so their worktable should be clear. It's more likely than finding a blank space in here."

"Sure."

Jerry stood, catching a pile as it started to topple over. "See what I mean? It's this way, just down the hall."

Adam followed. He hadn't ventured farther than Jerry's office. The man had offered a tour before getting called away twice now. Did Jerry understand how much help he needed? There always seemed to be volunteers around—but then, they also always looked busy. Were there any other paid staff? There had to be, didn't there?

The common room was occupied by three men sitting in chairs around a small coffee table. Their heads were bowed and one man prayed aloud.

"Ah." Jerry jerked his head to the far side of the room. "If we're quiet, we won't disturb them. I forgot Marlin was starting a Bible study today."

At the table, Adam shook the plans out of the tube and unrolled them. "Okay, this is the ground floor. You said a small foyer with room for a security desk—to maximize space, that's about all there's room for here. Here's the door into the main space, divided into four classrooms on a center hall with stairs down at the end."

Jerry traced each space as Adam described them.

"Second floor." Adam slid the first floor plan out of the way and held down the corner that kept trying to roll back up. "The back third is the locker room type area. The rest of the space is dormitory style like you wanted. The architect figures you should be able to get three rows of ten bunks without too much problem. You could forgo the center row and keep things to the walls if you wanted to provide a bit more space to each resident."

Jerry nodded. "We'll probably do that, to start—not that it matters from the building aspect. But having the option to house that many is huge."

Adam smiled and moved the pages. "Third floor is basically the same as the second, so you have the option to split it by gender or have multiple floors of one, depending on your needs. Finally, the fourth floor. You mentioned a lack of space for families."

"We don't have a lot of them, but right now we can't do anything about housing except split them up." Jerry shrugged.

"Right. So with that in mind, we divided the space into six mini-apartments, with a small common area just off the stairs. They're basically just a sleeping area and a private bathroom, but each can sleep four, and it makes more sense for a family unit." Adam glanced over at Jerry. What was he thinking? Did he not like it? "We can change it, if that's not the direction you wanted to go. It just seemed like it might meet a need."

"No. It's...it's perfect. I'm trying to decide if it wouldn't be better to get rid of the shared common space and make each one a little roomier. Or trade out for a communal bathroom and again, maybe split bedrooms so the adults had some privacy." Jerry scratched his chin. "Can I think about it a little?"

"Sure. I steered away from the communal bathroom just because kids and adults sharing...when they're not *all* family...I thought that might have the potential for problems. Communal would be cheaper."

"Oh. That's a fair point. One I'm sure the board would've thought of." Jerry chuckled. "They keep me on my toes. And that's a good thing. We don't meet until next week, but the plans are on the top of the agenda. We've got someone working the permit office as well. I'm praying that everything will come together and you'll be able to get started in the next month."

"Sounds great. Let me know what I can do to help." Adam shuffled the plans back into a pile and re-rolled them. "I'll leave the tube here with you, so you can use them at the board meeting. The architect has a second copy, but try not to lose them."

Jerry laughed. "Got it. Can I ask you something before you go?"

"Sure."

"How are you affording this?"

Adam rubbed the back of his neck. It was a complicated answer. "Lassiter Brothers has been looking for a way to give back to the community."

"Uh-huh. But giving back is a discount on labor or a free toilet. Not everything you're doing to this building for the quote you gave us. I'm reasonably certain your quote doesn't even cover materials. Let alone labor."

It didn't. They must have been getting some bids in before Adam brought in his proposal. "Will you promise that this goes no further?"

Jerry nodded.

"What Lassiter Brothers isn't covering, I am. The company's doing really well. Unlike my brothers, I don't have a wife and family to support. I still share an apartment with a roommate. Not because I have to, but because it just makes sense. I don't see the point in rattling around in a house all by myself, especially when I do hope to get married one day and I imagine my wife will want to have a say in where we live." Adam shrugged. "I save a lot of my profits...this just seemed like a really good place to spend some. And it's not as if you're getting it for free. The bill to the mission will still be hefty."

"Yeah, well...I hope you know how much it's appreciated. And it will be for many years to come." Jerry shook his head. "Thank you."

Heat flared on Adam's cheeks. "Don't mention it. Seriously."

Jerry laughed. "All right. Thanks for the plans. I'll get in touch as soon as the board is done deliberating and...then what?"

"Permits, if they're not already in place. After permits, I'll work up a schedule, line up subcontractors, and we'll get the project rolling." All the little details that he'd need to take care of zipped through Adam's mind, like they did at the beginning of any new project. But this time there was a subtle undercurrent of satisfaction that came with them.

Now that this was out of the way, he had an hour or so to get ready before he was picking up Sara. He'd found a dinner theater nearby that was putting on *South Pacific*. It seemed like something Sara would enjoy. And he'd enjoy being with her. Everyone wins.

16

"You don't have to walk me up." Sara pushed open the door to Adam's truck and hopped out. "I had a lot of fun tonight, though."

"I know I don't have to, but I can't help myself." Adam grinned and hit the lock button on his key fob. He met her at the front of the car and held out his hand. "Humor me?"

Sara laughed and slipped her fingers through his. "All right. Did you like the musical?"

"I didn't hate it."

"That's not really a ringing endorsement."

"I liked being with you."

She smiled up at him. "Smooth talker."

"Now there's something no one's ever accused me of before." He squeezed her fingers. "But I'll take it."

Sara poked the button for the elevator. "I enjoyed it. Even if the food wasn't five star restaurant worthy. The singing was good and the acting wasn't tragic."

Adam snorted. "Talk about ringing endorsements. I'll try and find something better next time."

She bumped his hip with hers. "I said it was fun. It was a good idea. Thank you."

"You're welcome."

They were quiet while the elevator finished going up to her floor. It was nice to be able to just *be*, without having to fill the air with needless chatter. She leaned her head on his shoulder for a moment before the doors opened. "Do you want to come in? I can probably scare up a soda. Maybe some cookies?"

"I should go. It's late."

Her heart sank. It was probably the right decision, but Sara wasn't ready for the night to end. "Okay."

Adam stopped in front of her door. After she'd unlocked it, he pulled her close and traced a finger down her cheek. "I want to come in. I just think it's smarter not to."

Mouth dry, Sara nodded. Her heart hammered in her chest. Was he going to kiss her? Her lips tingled in anticipation. And yet, as nice as kissing Adam would be, would she be able to stop? She hadn't had any kind of relationship since Luc. Hadn't wanted to trust herself—trust a man. Her tongue darted between her lips as his gaze captured hers.

His hand curved around her neck and he leaned closer.

Sara took a step back. She couldn't do this. Her hand clenched on the doorknob and wrenched it to the side. "I should go. Good night."

She caught the briefest flash of surprise and hurt on his face before she turned, fled through the door, and shut it in his face.

What had she done?

Sara stared at the ceiling and mentally kicked herself the same way she'd done all night. She'd managed a few minutes of sleep, when exhaustion simply overwhelmed her, but most of the night had been spent hiding under her pillow wondering what on earth she'd done.

A kiss. One simple kiss.

It could've been simple, couldn't it? She sighed. When was the last time she'd had a kiss that was? Too long to recall. And yet...Adam was different. He wasn't going to push.

It wasn't Adam she didn't trust. It was her.

Someone banged on her door.

Sara rolled over and frowned at the clock. Almost eleven. Had she promised to be somewhere? With Jen married and off on her honeymoon, it wasn't likely to be Rebecca trying to drag her out shopping again. After last night, it was unlikely Adam was ever going to speak to her, let alone come looking for her.

Maybe if she ignored whoever it was they'd go away.

More knocking.

Okay. Not going away. With a sigh, Sara threw off the covers, dragged a hand through her hair, and padded down the hall. She looked through the peep hole and furrowed her brow.

"Molly?"

"Hi. Can I come in? I brought coffee."

Coffee. The word was like a siren call. Sara undid the locks and tugged open the door. "Why?"

Molly laughed. "'Cause coffee is never a bad idea." She paused and raised her eyebrows. "Did I wake you?"

"I wasn't asleep." Sara shut the door and gestured toward the couch. "Have a seat."

"Here, drink this." Molly thrust an enormous paper cup at her. "I wasn't sure what you liked, so I just got two of what I get. I'll apologize in advance if you hate it."

Sara sniffed before taking a long swig. It was sweeter than what she usually drank and full of...caramel? But it wasn't bad. "It's fine. Thanks. So...?"

Molly settled on a sofa. "You doing okay?"

Sara sat, tucking her legs under her. Obviously, this wasn't going to be a quick conversation, for all that she'd talked to the woman maybe six times in her life. She was nice, that wasn't a question, but Sara wasn't one hundred percent convinced that Molly and Adam weren't supposed to end up together. "Sure. You?"

"I, ah, happened to be at Adam's when he got home last night."

Heat burned across her cheeks. Of course she had. "I take it Adam had a lot to say?"

"Surprisingly, no. But I'm pretty good at reading him, and he's hurt and upset and since he wouldn't talk about it, I thought I might see if you would." Molly cleared her throat. "I realize it's none of my business, but you're the first woman he's been interested in for a long time. And for what it's worth, I think you're a good match."

"How would you know?" Sara winced. "Sorry. That came out wrong. But...it's still valid. You don't really know me. I'm sure you know plenty about me. You've got ears."

"I have eyes, too." Sara must have looked confused, because Molly continued. "Look, sure, I've heard the rumors. But I've also seen you doing everything you can to distance yourself from that crowd. I believe in second chances."

Second chances. "Does Adam?"

"I don't think he would've asked you out if he didn't." Molly frowned. "Is that what this is about?"

Sara shook her head. Why had she asked? "Not because of my past. He and I have talked about that. Sort of. Last night, though..."

"Did you have a fight? Help me understand."

Sara sighed and stared at the top of her coffee. She barely knew Molly. Was it possible she'd understand? *Sara* didn't really understand. But what were her options? Jen was out of town. Rebecca was busy with the baby and Ben. Paige and Amy...they weren't close. Sara only talked to them when the whole group got together, and that hardly ever happened now. Besides, Jen and Rebecca would both give her the lecture about how she wasn't tied to her past anymore, she was a new creation. No condemnation. And that was good—better than good. But it wasn't helpful.

"Or not. I realize you don't know me." Molly stood. "I'm sorry. I shouldn't have barged in. I don't always think things all the way through. And, well, I care about Adam. I want to see him happy."

"I panicked." Sara chewed on her lower lip. "When you boil it all down, that's all it was. Panic."

Sara lowered herself back down to the couch. "Why?"

"He was going to kiss me."

"And you're not attracted to him?"

"No, it's not that. I am. How could someone not be?"

Molly drew her eyebrows together. "Then what's the problem?"

"Me. I'm the problem. Kissing...I love kissing. I love everything about it. And that's always how it starts."

"How it...oh."

Sara sighed. "Yeah. Oh."

"I think you need to give Adam more credit. He's not the kind of guy who's going to take advantage of a situation."

"What if I am?" It wasn't as if she'd been dragged unwillingly into her lifestyle before. She'd gone into every so-called relationship with her eyes wide open. "What if there's something inherent in me that's going to drag him down?"

"Now I think maybe you need to give yourself more credit." Molly shook her head. "I'm honestly not sure what to say, other than this: you and Adam make a good couple and I'd hate to see you let Satan use your past to ruin that."

Were they a good couple? She liked being around him. They had good conversations—better than she'd had with anyone before. They were friends first. The attraction was there, too. No question. But even if it wasn't, she'd still want to hang out with him. Sara sighed. "Is that what I did?"

"I can't say for sure, but from where I'm sitting? It sounds like it."

Sara nodded slowly. Maybe Molly had a point. That didn't tell her what to do about it, of course, but life was never as easy as she wished it was. "I'll think about that."

"*Pray* about it, too." Molly smiled. "And talk to Adam."

Sara winced and her stomach twisted into knots. Talk to Adam. If sinkholes developed where they should and swallowed people whole like they were supposed to, she wouldn't have to do that.

Molly chuckled. "It won't be that bad."

"Promise?"

"Nope. But he's not the kind of guy who's going to make you grovel. So that's something."

Yeah. Although, groveling was the least of her worries. "Thanks."

"Anytime." Molly leaned back, her gaze darting around the room. "Have any plans for your Saturday?"

Plans for the day that was almost half over? "I should clean the apartment."

"Pfft. You can do that any day. Wanna grab lunch and, I don't know, get a pedicure or something?"

Did she? Sara cocked her head to the side and studied Molly. It was a friendship overture, she recognized that. But why? Because she genuinely wanted to get to know Sara, or was it something else? She bit back a groan, when had she become so cynical? "Sure. Why not? Make yourself comfortable. I'll go get ready."

Sara sagged against the elevator wall and smiled. She'd had a good time, but goodness, Molly could go. After lunch, they'd gotten pedicures. While sitting with their feet in bubbling hot water, Molly had suggested heading to Great Falls. It hadn't seemed like a dumb idea at the time, but scrambling over not-quite-icy rocks while a colder-than-expected breeze blew at them off the river had made it clear that sunny day or not, February was not the time to hike. When they were finished, nothing would do but to grab another bite to eat before Molly dropped Sara back at her building.

Now she wanted to take a hot shower and crawl into bed. Her lack of sleep had caught up with her before they even got to the trail, and she'd been running on rapidly dissipating fumes ever since.

The elevator dinged, and the doors opened. Sara dug in her purse for her key and strode down the hall, steps faltering as she neared her door and saw someone leaning against it.

"Adam?"

He offered a weak smile and pushed to his feet, dusting off his jeans. "Hi. I was hoping maybe we could talk?"

So much for a shower and bed. She could say no, but that would send the wrong impression. It wasn't that she didn't want to talk to him—she did. They needed to. She'd just planned to do it at church tomorrow. Or after church. Sara unlocked the door and pushed it open.

"Come on in." She hung her coat in the closet and offered him a hangar before kicking off her sneakers and curling her toes. "Can I get you anything?"

He shook his head and reached around her to hang up his coat.

Sara moved into the living room and sat, tucking her feet under her. "I'm sorry."

Adam studied her for several heartbeats before nodding and settling far enough away on the couch that they didn't touch.

At least he didn't sit on the other side of the room. That was good, wasn't it? Sara swallowed. Did she have to start the conversation? Probably. The awkwardness was her fault. She cleared her throat. "You probably figured out that I panicked."

"I wasn't sure what it was."

She closed her eyes. She really had hurt him. "I'm sorry."

"You said that."

Sara laughed.   "Okay. Well. Still true. But panic. Not...disinterest."

"You're sure?" He scooted a little closer, his expression earnest. "Because if you don't feel the same way about me as I do about you...I don't want...we don't have to...we can just be friends."

Her heart sped up, the sound like a rushing waterfall in her head. Tears pricked her eyes. "I don't want that. I mean, we are friends. I like being friends. I don't want to *just* be friends."

His hand closed over hers, its warmth soothing. "Okay. What do you want?"

She turned and met his gaze. "This. I want this."

Sara took a deep breath and leaned close, brushing her lips across his. Even that little contact sent electricity zinging. She wanted more. Instead, she sat back, and squeezed his hand.

His face was unreadable. Should she not have kissed him? Was he angry? Maybe...her stomach sank...maybe he hadn't felt anything. Her voice was a whispery croak. "Say something."

"I'm trying to decide what to do."

"What do you mean?"

He took her face in his hands and rested his forehead on hers. "I'd like to do that again. Properly. I also don't want to scare you off."

She let out a nervous chuckle.

"So here's the thing, I promise that I will never push you. And I also promise that kissing is it, until we're married."

Married? He saw her as someone he could marry? Sara blinked back tears.

"Hey. Don't cry. I'm not..."

"I'm tired. I'm just tired. I didn't sleep last night because I was so worried I'd ruined everything. I'm really glad I didn't." Sara let out a shuddering breath.

Adam pulled her into his arms and rubbed her back. "I'll head home. See you tomorrow at church?"

Sara nodded, her face buried in his chest. She inhaled his subtle woodsy sent and sighed. "I don't want you to go."

He nudged her head up so his gaze met hers and smiled. "Maybe I can stay a few minutes?"

His intent was obvious. Sara had only a moment to worry before his lips met hers and everything else faded away.

Adam whistled as he parked his truck in the visitor parking of Sara's building. It was a beautiful spring evening—maybe he could talk her into skipping prayer meeting and going for a picnic somewhere. They could pick up a bucket of chicken and sit out and enjoy the mid-April weather, and the break in the rain they'd had so far this week.

He pushed the elevator button, nodding to one of the other residents of her building. Over the last two months, he'd started to recognize several people who lived here from his visits to collect Sara for church on Sundays and Wednesdays and weekend dates. Realistically, he was here four days a week for one reason or another—sometimes the reasons were completely fabricated. Sara never seemed to mind.

Sara's door swung open before he could knock. "You're late. I was just thinking about worrying."

"Am I? Sorry. I was down at the mission today and didn't get out as ahead of the traffic as I'd hoped." Adam reached for her hand as she pulled the door closed and leaned closer to brush a kiss across her cheek. He'd much rather take her in his arms and kiss her properly, but...Sara was pretty strict about that. He understood it, mostly. But that didn't mean he had to like it.

"It's all right. I was running behind, myself. So at least I didn't keep you waiting." She chuckled. "How's the new building going?"

"Smoothest project I've worked on. I'm guessing because so many people are praying for it. Honestly, the inspection today was the first one I've ever been part of where there wasn't *something* that had to be corrected."

"You got the go-ahead?"

Adam nodded. "Drywall will start going up tomorrow. If things keep moving at this rate, we should have occupancy by the middle of next month."

"Wow." Sara reached for the handle to the passenger door, beating Adam by a fraction of a second. "That's great."

"It really is." He waited until she was seated before closing the door and heading to his own side. "So. Do you really want to go to prayer meeting?"

Sara furrowed her brow. "Why wouldn't I? Why wouldn't you?"

"Because it's a gorgeous evening and we're young and in—" Adam stopped himself, mentally backtracking. In love? Oh yeah. But he wasn't ready to tell her. Or, more to the point, it didn't seem like she was ready to hear it. "Interesting."

"Young and interesting?" Sara laughed. "That's a new one. What were you thinking?"

"Picnic at the park?"

"Why don't we do that this weekend, when we have more time? In fact, I've been hoping to get downtown to see the last dribbles of cherry blossoms. We could go walk around the tidal basin and picnic on the Mall."

The cherry blossoms were mostly gone. If it rained again between now and the weekend, they'd completely disappear. Still, a picnic downtown would be fun. They hadn't done that yet. The two times he'd planned something along those lines, the weather hadn't cooperated. "Sure, okay. How was your day?"

"Not as amazing as your seamless inspection, but not bad. You remember I have the mission trip meeting afterward tonight, right?"

He hadn't remembered that. She usually tried to talk him into meeting her there when they were getting together. He always resisted. Maybe she'd given up. He didn't mind waiting. If they came separately, he didn't get a chance to have supper with her, and he looked forward to that from the time he dropped her off on Sunday afternoon. "Right."

"You forgot."

He shrugged. "It's fine. I have my laptop, I can do paperwork."

"You really should let me drive myself. We're going to be meeting every week until we leave, making sure everything is planned and ready."

Adam nodded. The youth trip had been like that, too. Honestly, he'd been glad when it was time to leave simply because it brought an end to the constant meetings. "It's fine. I don't mind. And I'm not ready to sacrifice any of my time with you."

She grinned and reached for his hand. "If you change your mind, let me know. It's really not a problem for me to drive."

"Got it." He pulled into a parking spot at church and cut the engine. She was so independent. This was a good thing, most of the time. But...would it kill her to act like she needed him even a tiny bit? Maybe need was the wrong word, but he couldn't put his finger on the right one. He counted hours between their dates, sending her texts just because or calling when he knew she had a break. Sara...did none of that. She was warm when they were together—sometimes more than warm when he could sneak past her initial defenses and actually kiss her lips. Then it was clear she wasn't indifferent to him. But she didn't seem to crave him the way he did her.

He didn't consider himself someone who had self-esteem issues...but he loved her. And he couldn't tell her, because he wasn't sure how she'd react. It was starting to get old.

"No date tonight? On a Friday?" Molly dropped her purse on the kitchen table and kicked off her shoes before ambling to the living room and stretching out on the sofa.

"Make yourself at home." Adam shook his head and began gathering the pile of papers he'd spread out all over the coffee table. "I'll be out of your way in a few."

Molly frowned. "What's going on?"

"Nothing. Don't worry about it. Karl said he'd be back soon—he ran out to get...something. I don't really remember what."

"Yeah, he texted me. You didn't answer either of my questions."

"No. And nothing. Which I believe I did answer." Adam sighed and stood, papers in his arms. "You two have fun."

"What if I am worried about it?"

Adam kept walking down the hall. There was no way he was going to talk to Molly about it. Last time he'd done that, she'd gone over to talk to Sara, and that was the last thing he needed happening. Ever. He would figure this out on his own or talk to his girlfriend himself. Not that that was likely to go over super well. He'd tried, sort of, to broach the issue on Wednesday while they ate after her mission trip meeting. She'd been preoccupied, though, so maybe it wasn't all him. Maybe it was bad timing?

"Adam."

He turned and blinked to see Molly so close behind him. "Sometimes you're like a dog with a bone, you know that?"

"I don't consider that a bad thing. Are you okay?"

He went into his room and dropped the papers on his desk. He'd worry about the contract revisions this new potential client wanted later. Their lawyer hadn't seen an issue with them, but his brothers wanted Adam to go through and summarize the changes in layman's terms. Because the lawyers had done a less-than-optimal job at that. "I don't know. Probably."

"Wanna talk about it?"

What part of no was she not getting? He stared at her.

Molly hunched her shoulders. "Okay, I know you don't *want* to talk about it. Think maybe you should anyway?"

"Not really."

She huffed out a breath. "We aren't friends now that I'm dating Karl? Is that it?"

"We're friends, Moll, I just don't need you running off to talk to Sara. I don't really understand why you did that in February, and I don't need you doing it now. If you two were longstanding friends, I'd sort of get it. But you hardly know each other, and I don't need you meddling."

"Wow." Her tone turned icy. "I didn't realize helping you out was such a burden. It won't happen again."

Adam watched her stomp down the hallway and groaned. Great. Just great. But what was he supposed to do? What he'd said wasn't wrong, and okay, sure, she was trying to help, but...was he supposed to chase her down and apologize? That'd be a lot easier to swallow if she'd even been the tiniest bit sorry for butting in last time.

Whatever. They'd figure it out later. Probably. And if they didn't, well...Molly hadn't had much time for him since she and Karl got together anyway. He hadn't really made time for her, either. Between Sara and work, he didn't have a lot of free time. Maybe he should talk to Sara about going on a double date with them. Half the time it seemed like Molly and Karl spent their time together playing video games, but they'd probably go somewhere if they were invited, wouldn't they?

Adam checked the time on his phone. Sara was over at Ben and Rebecca's. Or was it Jen and David's? Didn't matter. She was with friends, and he was supposed to be summarizing these contract changes. She...he ought to stop worrying about Molly, and Sara for that matter, and focus on work. Then it'd be off his plate, and hopefully out of his mind, when he and Sara went on a picnic tomorrow.

The crash of thunder outside his window shattered Adam's sleep. He rolled over and listened to the rain pounding against the side of his apartment building. The alarm on his clock began to chime quietly as a flash of lightning shone through the blinds on his window. The rumble of thunder wasn't far behind.

Adam sat up and stretched his arms over his head. Was it raining like this downtown? Sometimes the suburbs got the storms and the city stayed dry. He reached for his phone, silenced the alarm, and opened the weather app. No such luck today. The radar for the entire area was covered by the enormous storm system. They were predicting up to six inches of rain in some places, so even after it moved on the ground wasn't going to be very good for picnics.

With a sigh, he shuffled down the hall. He'd get breakfast and then figure out what to do. He could go back to bed. He'd only set an alarm so he had plenty of time to put the picnic together. But at this point, he was up.

"Morning." Karl rubbed his eyes in the doorway to his room. "Some storm."

"Yeah." In the kitchen, Adam took down a box of cereal and a bowl. Should he suggest a movie instead? What was even playing in the theater right now? They didn't do a lot of dinner-and-a-movie-dates, so it could still fit the novelty box. Sort of. He filled the bowl and tucked the box back in its place.

"Weren't you heading downtown today?" Karl opened the fridge and stared inside.

"That was the plan. Not thinking that's going to pan out. What'd you and Molly do last night? You were quiet."

"We went out." Karl closed the fridge and grabbed a banana out of the bowl on the table. "She said you needed to be alone."

Adam snorted.

"Sounds like she wasn't wrong. Wanna talk about it?"

"Nope."

"Okay." Karl tossed the banana peel in the general direction of the trashcan, grinning when it landed on the edge and stayed there, hanging over the side. "So what will you do instead of going downtown?"

"That's what I was working on."

"Hmm. You could still go. Museums'll be dry inside. It's just getting from the parking to the door that'll stink."

"We were going to have a picnic near the Tidal Basin, see some of the last of the cherry blossoms, walk around."

"Oh. Yeah, that's out. And those blossoms are history if it's pounding downtown like it is here."

Going to a museum was a thought. Of course, the aforementioned soaking getting inside was still a factor. There wasn't any good parking nearby and the Metro station was in the center of the Mall. It was impossible to get anywhere and still stay dry. "I don't know. The wet has to factor in."

Karl nodded. "Why not picnic here? Or at her place?"

"I'm not following. You remember the storm, right?"

"Sure, but it's not inside. Move the furniture out of the way, spread out a blanket, and voila, indoor picnic."

That...might work. Adam pursed his lips. Would Sara go for it? It meant being alone and unchaperoned, and that was likely to be a deal breaker. "I guess I can ask."

"You don't think she'd go for it?"

He hadn't really talked to Karl about the physical aspect of his relationship with Sara. "I kind of figured Molly had filled you in."

"About?"

Adam poked the cereal in his bowl before spooning up a bite. "She's...really not happy when we're alone."

"What? That's crazy. Why not?"

"It's not crazy. I get it. I don't like it. But I get it. You know her history, right?" At Karl's nod, Adam continued, "She's worried— bordering on terrified—that things will get out of control."

"Hmm."

Whatever that meant. Adam turned his attention to his cereal. Would he be able to talk her into a picnic at her apartment? Or should he just invite her over here? "Did you have plans to go out today?"

"Nah. I should be around."

"I guess I'll see if she wants to come here, then. Can you make yourself kind of scarce though?"

Karl grinned. "I'll stay in my room. Okay if I move the game console in there?"

"Absolutely." He took another bite and chewed while he worked out the preparations, but his thoughts strayed to the few kisses he and Sara had shared. "Can I ask you a question that has the potential to be weird?"

Karl laughed. "How do I say no to a lead-in like that? Hit me."

"You and Molly kiss, right?"

"Uh, yeah?"

"And neither of you have felt the need to slam the brakes on so hard that you get whiplash?"

Karl cleared his throat. "There have been a couple of occasions when it's been tempting—really tempting—to do more than just kiss. But we've talked about our intentions to honor God so much, it's not as hard to stop as I think it might otherwise be. Add in the fact that I'm pretty sure she'd deck me if I *did* try..."

Adam snickered. "There's that."

Karl shrugged. "Plus, I love her. I told her that last night for the first time. I'm fairly certain she's the one."

"Wow. Congrats, man."

"She's still mulling it over, but I think she'll come around. I'm not in a rush."

Adam wasn't really in a rush himself. Sure, he'd always imagined he'd get married right out of college, but it wasn't as if twenty-eight was ancient. There was still time...although he'd like to be married by thirty.

"I can see your gears grinding." Karl tipped back on the back two legs of his chair.

"Just doing the math. I was thinking I wasn't in a hurry, either. Except I'd kind of like to be married—settled—in the next two years. That's not actually all that much time."

"The big three-oh, huh? I'm with you. But having seen my sister rush into marriage because of a looming birthday, struggle through those vows as she uncovered just how wrong they were together, and then fight through a painful divorce...I'm working hard to keep age from being a factor."

"I forgot about your sister." Adam frowned. "She doing any better?"

"Not really. Now that she's divorced, she's convinced that God will never forgive her, even though she fought with everything in her to keep their marriage together. It was him who walked. And the church...isn't super encouraging. She feels like she's walking around with a big sign on her back that says 'Warning! Divorcee!' on it."

"She and Sara should talk. Sara's convinced everyone still holds her sins against her. Do you think...I just can't...why would people do that? Don't they realize they're sinners too?"

Karl shook his head. "Sure, but they figure they've only done the little sins, not the big ones. It helps them feel superior. More righteous."

"And that just *proves* they don't listen to Pastor Brown. How many sermons has he done where he's mentioned that there aren't such things as big and little sins?"

"I hear you, and I totally agree. I think it's human nature though, man. We're all looking for ways to feel better about ourselves, and putting someone else down always provides that quick fix. Or so it seems. Plus, sin that has to do with sex? That's got some juice to it, you know?"

"Yeah, yeah." Adam lifted his bowl and drank the milk along with the last few bites of cereal that floated in it. "I guess I ought to see if I can talk Sara into the indoor picnic thing."

"If she's not game, let me know. I'd just as soon not unhook the electronics if I don't have to."

"Got it." Adam set his bowl in the sink and went back down the hallway, lining up the arguments he'd use. Karl being home was good. Of course, he'd been hoping for the illusion of privacy that being out on the Mall provided. He sighed and unplugged his cell phone. Either way he got to see and be near her. That was worth it. Even if it did sign him up for sappy status.

18

Sara pushed her empty plate to the center of the checkered blanket and grinned at Adam. "This was fun. When I heard the rain this morning I was so disappointed."

"I'm glad it worked out. I can't take the credit though, it was Karl's idea."

She moved closer and brushed her lips across Adam's, savoring the subtle thrill that always came when they touched. She ached for more, and that had her jerking away just as his arms came around her. Sara cleared her throat. "You'll have to thank him for me."

Adam pressed his lips together in a thin line and nodded.

"Please don't be angry."

"I'm not angry." He reached for her plate and stacked it on his, avoiding her eyes as he began to tidy up their feast.

She'd ruined it. Again. "I'm sorry."

"Don't." His gaze jerked up and connected with hers. "That just makes it worse."

She swallowed and watched him rise and carry the dishes and food to the kitchen. What was she supposed to do? Part of her wanted to let her own anger loose. This wasn't easy for her and it didn't seem unreasonable to expect him to understand that. And yet...their relationship wasn't like most normal relationships. Even normal relationships amongst the small number of people in their acquaintance who managed to keep true to God's expectations before marriage.

That had been one of the things she'd finally broached with her girlfriends last night—not that that had been awkward or anything. Sara had known they'd kissed, obviously, but she'd finally needed to know just how much kissing they'd done. It had been...surprising. How had they managed to make out without crossing lines? Their answers hadn't been entirely satisfactory. Pray together. Talk things out. Pray some more. It had to be harder than that, didn't it?

Adam returned and sat on the far side of the blanket, leaning against the sofa he'd pushed against the wall to make room for their picnic. "Do you need me to take you home?"

"No. I want to stay. I want to spend time with you. This week is going to be crazy—I'm putting in extra hours and we have two different mission team meetings. We have to be at the airport at four a.m. on Saturday and then I'm out of town for two weeks. This is kind of our last chance to be alone for a while." She scooted next to him and laid her head on his shoulder.

He snaked his arm around her, pulling her close, and pressed a kiss to her forehead. "Okay. Movie? I have a bunch we can choose from."

A movie. Wouldn't it be nice to snuggle up with him on the couch and just be? They didn't do a lot of that—hardly any if she was honest—because she was bound and determined to keep them from straying the way she had in the past. His roommate was home. It was the middle of the day. Surely it wouldn't be a bad idea. "That sounds just about perfect."

"I love you."

Sara's head jerked up, eyes wide. Her mouth went dry. Where had that come from?

"I'm sorry." Adam's cheeks were red and he shifted away, turning so he could face her. "I wasn't going to tell you yet. I was going to wait at least until after you got back from the trip. I know you don't need any pressure or stress right now, so don't feel like you have to say anything. I just...thought you should know. I'll go get my movies."

She watched as he stood and padded down the hall, her thoughts churning. He loved her? It left her warm all the way through, like she'd been tucked up in a quilt by the fire. Cozy. She'd had the words said to her before. She'd even said them back. But none of those times were like this. For the first time, the emotion behind the words might actually be real instead of a means to an end.

But how did she know for sure?

Adam came back carrying a fat binder and settled down next to her, opening the case in his lap. "They're arranged by genre, then alphabetically within that. So if you have a type of movie in mind, let's start there."

Sara snickered. "How long did this take you?"

"Not that long. Especially once it's set up. Sometimes adding a new movie calls for a bit of rearranging, but...you're making fun of me."

"Just a little. You're right though, this makes sense." Anal. Who knew the guy was this anal? He probably preferred the word "organized," but honestly. It was kind of adorable. "Got anything with aliens?"

"Do I ever." Adam grinned and flipped pages. "Here we go. Pick your poison."

Sara flipped a couple of pages before tapping a disc. "This one."

"Good pick." He slid the disc out of the sleeve and started to stand.

"I love you, too." Sara held her breath and shot up a quick prayer as she finished saying the words. Was she doing the right thing? It felt right. But how was she supposed to *know*? To trust herself? Trust Adam?

He eased back down beside her. "Really?"

Her heart hammered in her chest as she nodded.

He used a finger to trace her jaw. Eyes locked with hers, he leaned forward.

Sara's tongue darted between her lips. Trust. She could trust Adam. And herself. Already they'd stayed on the straight and narrow longer than any relationship she'd had. One kiss, one *real* kiss, wasn't going to undo that.

Sara's eyes drifted closed as their lips touched. She sighed and sank into Adam's embrace.

Sara zipped the top of her suitcase closed. It was only Thursday, but she was packed. One more long day at work and then two weeks in Jamaica. Not that there'd be any of the relaxing on the beach like her vacation after Christmas. The mission committee had stuffed the schedule with activities. Between medical clinics and outreach, they'd be working every day. Somehow, Sara had ended up on a team doing abstinence education for teens and young adults. Her stomach clenched. God had a funny sense of humor.

The knock at her door made her frown. It was after eight. Her plan was to read for an hour and get to bed early. There was no point in starting everything off exhausted—or more exhausted than usual. Sleeping on the plane wasn't going to happen, she'd found that out in December. Seeing Adam through the peephole made her smile.

She opened the door. "What are you doing here?"

"I decided I couldn't let you leave without seeing you one more time. I know tomorrow night you need to get to bed, and you probably need to pack, but I hoped maybe you had a few minutes?"

"Come on in. I'm actually packed. Just finished. I was planning on reading, but seeing you is definitely better."

He grinned and pulled her into his arms, resting his cheek against her head. "I'll miss you."

"It's only two weeks. You'll probably be so busy you hardly notice I'm gone."

Adam snorted. "Right. Although the sheetrock is going well downtown, so maybe we'll get into all the finishing minutia. That always takes a little more concentration than the big scheduling jobs. More to oversee."

"See?" She smiled and stepped back. "Want some coffee? I have decaf."

"Yeah? I'd like that."

Sara wound her fingers through his and tugged as she started toward the kitchen. "Make yourself at home."

Adam sat at the kitchen table while she put the kettle on the stove and ground some beans.

While they waited for the water to boil, Sara sat across from him and took his hand. "For what it's worth, I'm going to miss you, too. I didn't mean to be dismissive. It's just the tape I've been playing in my head the last few days—it's only two weeks."

He smiled. "That helps. I was starting to worry."

The kettle whistled. Sara rose and flicked off the burner before pouring the boiling water over the coffee grounds in her French press. "So what do you have lined up while I'm gone?"

"Other than the mission building? We finally got the contracts all sorted for a new build out near Leesburg. It's a really nice custom job on a great plot. Four acres, fairly wooded. And the family wants to keep as many trees as they can. It makes a bigger challenge, but I always love the end result better than when we just go in and flatten—or when a subdivision has already had it done. So we'll probably start on-site prep for that. Then I have a handful of other builds at various stages. They're running smoothly, but you still have to keep on top of them to make sure it stays that way." Adam shrugged. "Business as usual, basically."

"And the weekend?"

"Try to avoid Molly and Karl, mostly. They're right on the border of too cute for words. It's a little nauseating."

Sara laughed and slowly pressed the plunger that pushed all the coffee grounds to the bottom of the carafe, leaving the dark brew behind. "But you're glad she's happy, right?"

"Of course. And while I'm still scratching my head a little— they aren't necessarily the most obvious couple to me—they're starting to seem natural. Karl's already thinking of proposing. Except you can't say anything about that."

"That's...fast. Isn't that fast?" Sara poured two cups of coffee.

Adam reached for his and sipped. "I don't know. They've known each other forever. Maybe they've only been dating a few months, but it's not like they were strangers."

"Hmm." Sara stirred sugar into her coffee before she sipped. It still seemed fast to her. On the other hand, if Adam were to propose...she'd probably say yes. Her breath caught in her lungs. Wow. Where had that thought come from?

"And they're not kids, either. I think when you're older—out of college and on your own for several years—there's something to be said for...I don't know, accelerating the timeline a little. Not without a ton of prayer, obviously, but the friends for two years before you start dating for two years and then get engaged right before you graduate thing that seems pretty wise in college sounds like overkill when you're tiptoeing toward thirty."

That was reasonable. He wasn't advocating for jumping in without a lot of thought and prayer. "Prayer is definitely a necessary part if you're bumping up the timeline."

"Even if you aren't." He squeezed her hand. "I pray for you and about us every day. I guess maybe I haven't mentioned that and I should have. When I told you I love you, it wasn't hasty. It's something I've done a lot of thinking and praying about."

"I...need to be better about that. Maybe we could do it together?" Of course, she was leaving for Jamaica, so how did that work?

"Absolutely. I'd like that. You can get text messages while you're gone, right?"

"I have an app. Hang on." She dug her phone out of her pocket and scrolled through until she found it. She turned it so he could see and pointed. "If you get that too, we can send messages for free. I think it even does audio messages."

"Cool." Adam slipped out his phone and tapped the screen. "There it is. And...got it. Sent you a connection request."

Sara's phone chimed. She tapped the screen with a grin. "We're set."

Adam tipped his coffee cup and set it down empty. "I should probably let you go."

"I'm glad you came over." Sara stood and moved around the table, settling on his lap before he could stand. She ignored the electricity that sparkled through her and wound her arms around his neck, lowering her forehead to his. "I love you."

His arms wrapped around her and he tipped his face up, his lips brushing hers. "I love you, too. Be safe."

Sara nodded and, ignoring the tiny voice of fear and distrust that tried to get her attention, adjusted the angle of her head so she could give him a proper goodbye kiss.

19

"You made it." Adam's sister-in-law Carol wrapped Adam in a tight hug. "The kids are going to be so excited. They've been pestering me all week to know if Uncle Adam was going to make it. Your brother wasn't sure."

"Sorry." Adam tucked his hands in his pockets. "I guess I should've let you know sooner."

"Don't worry about it. Aaron and Asher are both out back with the kids. They've already got the grill going."

"Did Francesca make it?"

Carol shook her head. "She packed a bag and walked out yesterday. Asher thinks she went to her parents."

Adam winced. "How's Asher?"

"About how you'd expect, I guess. We're really praying her parents send her right back home. Right now, the kids just think she needed to see her mom—a little mini vacation, you know? I don't know what'll happen if she doesn't change her mind and he has to explain that their mom doesn't want to be their mom anymore." Carol patted his arm. "Go on out. It's good you came."

Nodding, Adam wound his way through his eldest brother's gorgeous home. It was one of their first projects. None of them had been thinking of making a business out of it, but they'd discovered an aptitude and enjoyment that, when everything was added up, made sense. And so Lassiter Brothers was formed, all because of one custom build to try and get a dream house for an affordable price. It was probably still the house Adam loved the most. Maybe because it was the first.

He stepped through the French doors onto the deck that stretched across the entire back of the house, with a second level down below that could be reached through the basement or a staircase on one end. His brothers sat in chairs by the grill, feet propped on the rail and sodas in hand, while six kids ranging in age from four to ten ran around on the yard screeching with glee.

"Hey."

Asher and Aaron turned in unison, both grinned. Aaron pointed to an empty chair. "Pull up a seat and enjoy the bedlam."

Adam grabbed the chair and dragged it closer to his brothers. "You know you love it. Both of you."

"True enough." Asher took a long drink from his can. "Carol fill you in?"

"Sort of. Can I do anything to help?" Adam watched the kids playing, hoping that two of them weren't going to have their hearts broken in the coming weeks.

"Just pray. I still can't wrap my head around it. I thought we were doing okay. One day we're talking about what family vacation to plan for next summer, and the next she says needs to think and is packing a bag to head to her parents'. What happened is anyone's guess. She won't talk to me." Asher rubbed the back of his neck and sighed.

"Sorry, man." Adam watched smoke billow out of the grill. "Should someone check that?"

Aaron shook his head. "There's nothing in there yet, I'm cleaning it."

"Ah. I thought you were supposed to use that scraper and steel brush to do that."

Aaron shrugged. "This way works and it's less effort."

Asher chuckled. "You know Aaron and easier."

"That I do." Adam shook his head. "Thanks for inviting me over. It was nice to have some plans that got me away from Karl and Molly. I told you they're dating, right?"

"Your roommate and your best friend?" Asher frowned. "I don't think you did, actually. How's that working out?"

"Seems to be going well from what Karl's said. He's already thinking marriage." Adam still struggled with that idea, although

Molly had always said she wanted a big family, so it wasn't like she didn't need to get married first. Karl and Molly. He could wish them well, even if it caused a little pang in his own heart.

"And you?" Asher set his can down on the deck and folded his hands in his lap.

"What about me?"

"You going to ever do more than be fun Uncle Adam? Maybe contribute to the chaos with minions of your own?" Asher and Aaron exchanged a look. "Seems we recall hearing about there being a woman recently."

Heat spread across Adam's cheeks. "Sara's in Jamaica for two weeks on a mission trip."

"Aha. Now we know why you came." Aaron stood and opened the grill's lid. More smoke billowed out, causing everyone to cough. "There we go."

"Clean?" Asher moved to stand by Aaron at the grill. "Nice. I'll go get the burgers and dogs from Carol."

Aaron waited until Asher was inside before sighing. "He's not doing great."

"Why would he be?"

"True. What he didn't tell you is he's worried Francesca may be seeing someone else."

Lead settled in Adam's stomach. "Oh no."

"Yeah. He doesn't have any proof. Yet. But there have been enough little things that raised flags. We're going to keep the kids for the weekend so he has time to look around without having to try and explain what could be nothing."

Adam nodded. Poor Asher. "Should I offer to come help?"

Aaron shrugged. "Can't hurt. In the meantime, let him tease you about Sara, would you? It's good to see him relaxing."

"Sure thing. That's what younger brothers are for, right?" Adam rolled his eyes. It wasn't like he could stop either of his brothers for ragging on him. He'd never been able to do that. At this point in his life, he'd worry there was something wrong if they didn't give him grief. If there was a side bonus of cheering Asher up, well, so be it. "When are we going to eat? I'm starved."

Adam climbed the steps of his brother's house, a bag of takeout in his hand. He rang the bell and waited.

Asher pulled open the door and frowned. "Hey. Did I know you were coming over?"

"Nope. But I brought lunch."

His brother scrubbed a hand over his face and stepped back, opening the door wider. "Okay. Why?"

"Thought you might need some company." Adam wasn't quite as at home at Asher's as he was at Aaron's. They tended to congregate at the other house rather than here. Was that Francesca's preference? He was beginning to realize he didn't know his second sister-in-law as well as he thought. He never would've imagined her walking away from her kids. He passed through the large sunken living room to the kitchen and took a seat at the island. "How are you doing?"

"I don't even know how to answer that yet. I guess I'm numb." Asher took the stool next to him and reached into the paper bag. "Everything the same in here?"

"Yeah. Burgers, loaded, and a large fry. I figured we could share since they always dump in extra." Adam removed his own foil-wrapped burger and tore the brown paper sack down the middle to expose the peanut-oil fries.

"Hang on. I'm pretty sure there's malt vinegar in the pantry." Asher stood and crossed the kitchen. "Aaron called this morning, said the kids are doing okay. That's good. They all went to church...I couldn't make myself go. Did you?"

Adam nodded and unwrapped the enormous burger. Since Sara wasn't there, he'd gone to the singles class, having forgotten that Molly and Karl weren't attending it anymore. While he hadn't realized how banal it was when it was the only class he'd attended, going back...well, he wouldn't make that mistake again. "What'd you do instead?"

"Tried to pray. Ended up crying." Asher shrugged and set the bottle of vinegar on the counter. "I just don't understand this. Shouldn't I have seen it coming somehow?"

"Aaron said there might be someone else?"

"I don't know. I really hope not, but I'm so confused. I'm grasping at straws." He pushed his burger away and reached for a fry. "What am I going to do if she leaves me?"

"We'll get through it together. That's what Lassiters do. Right?"

"I guess."

Adam frowned as he ate. It was hard to see his brother like this. He looked...defeated. His shoulders slumped, and he was pale. Except for the circles under his eyes. Those were plenty dark. "What can I do to help?"

"I was thinking I might try to go through some of her papers and email, that kind of thing. But this morning, I got the feeling that I should just leave it alone."

"Why?" Wouldn't it be better to know? To find proof and confront her with it, or find nothing and have a little more peace of mind?

"I can't explain it. I told you I was trying to pray, right? I didn't have the words...it ended up really disjointed. I guess it's good God understands the heart. And I was in the office staring at her computer and it was almost like a physical hand pushed me away. So I left the room." Asher snagged another fry. "Every time I think about going back in there again, I get nauseous."

Weird. And also kind of cool. Even if it wasn't what he'd choose, Adam didn't see how to explain it other than God's intervention. "Okay. Then we leave it be. We could put on a movie, see if it gets your mind off things for a few minutes."

"Worth a try." Asher wrapped his burger back up. "I'll put this in the fridge. Unless you want it?"

"The days of me eating two of these monsters are long past."

Asher gave a weak smile. "You're getting old like the rest of us. Time for you to settle down. Do we get to meet your girl anytime soon?"

Sara. She'd been gone a little over twenty-four hours and he already missed her like crazy. She'd texted yesterday when they landed, but that was all he'd heard so far. Not surprising. The church down there was big on jumping in. Maybe she'd have some free time this afternoon or evening. "Maybe when she's back? I'll see what I can work out."

"So you are serious."

Adam nodded.

"Good. That's good. Marriage. A family. Those are things to work for. To cherish."

"Even now?"

"Especially now. I'm not giving up on us. Francesca wanted some space. Fine. She can have a few days. But then?" Asher smacked a fist into his other hand. "Then we're going to deal with...whatever this is. If she doesn't come home, I'll go there."

"And if she says there's no one else?"

"Then I trust her and we work through whatever is bothering her. Trust is hard sometimes, but without it, there's no point. Come on, I've got that new shoot 'em up everyone raved about last year."

They were about halfway through the movie when the light turned on.

"What..." Asher sat up and glanced over his shoulder then stilled. "Francesca."

"Hi. Um. I...can we talk?"

Adam cleared his throat and started to stand. "I'll get going."

"No, Adam. You might as well stay. I...you'd find out anyway." Francesca stepped into the room and crossed to a chair. "Could you turn that off?"

Asher hit the remote.

Adam glanced between his brother and sister-in-law. "I really think I should go. Let you two work this out."

Asher put his hand on Adam's arm. "If she says it's okay, then it's fine with me."

The air was thick. Adam wasn't sure who to look at. He wanted to shrink into a tiny ball and disappear, just like he'd wanted during the infrequent times his parents had fought when he was growing up.

"So. I guess I'll just...look, I don't want a divorce." Tears began to flow down Francesca's face. "I know that's probably what's going to happen, but I'm begging you to please, *please*, at least hear me out."

Asher nodded but said nothing.

Adam tried to stay as still as possible. He shouldn't be here. This was between his brother and his wife. He opened his mouth to excuse himself, but Francesca started talking before he could say anything.

"I told you when Mark looked me up on social media. You remember?"

"Two, three months ago, right?" Asher frowned. "What does that have to do with anything?"

Who was Mark? Adam slid down the couch. Maybe he could ease out of the room and no one would notice.

Francesca turned and pinned him in place with her gaze. "I dated Mark for most of high school. Was still dating him, though it was basically over, when I met your brother in college."

"Ah. I...still don't think I need to be here." Why did neither of them see how awkward this was for Adam? Not that it was about him. Obviously it wasn't. But still...didn't they want privacy?

"We exchanged some instant messages, caught up on life. It was nice. He's married, too. Has two kids. Does a lot of travelling for work, but enjoys getting home on the weekends. I don't know exactly when things changed. The tone of his messages got...flirty, I guess. And it felt good to know he still considered me attractive. I told myself there was nothing wrong with it. I love you, Asher. I love our kids. I thought I knew what I was doing." She wrung her hands in her lap as tears continued to drip off her cheeks.

"But? I'm guessing there's a but coming. You packed a bag and left, Frannie." Asher rubbed his hands on his thighs. Adam guessed he was fighting the urge to go to her. Asher wasn't one to sit by while the woman he loved was hurting.

Francesca wiped her cheeks and nodded. "We met for dinner. You were busy, and Carol was already picking the kids up from school, so it was easy to justify. Just a chance to see him while he was in town, say hi. I didn't sleep with him. But it was clear that's what he wanted...and I'm ashamed to say I was tempted."

"But you didn't." Asher did stand now and crossed the room, sinking to his knees in front of his wife. "Why did you leave?"

"I thought it would be easier to leave before you kicked me out." She buried her face in her hands. "I didn't know what else to do."

"You could have told me. Like you just did." Asher reached for her hand and pulled it away so he met her eyes. "I love you. This doesn't change that."

Francesca flung her arms around him and collapsed against his chest, sobbing.

Adam blinked back his own tears and tiptoed from the room. He clearly didn't need to be there anymore, but it was nice to know that a happy resolution looked possible. As he walked to his car, he dialed Aaron.

"You find something?"

"That's a nice way to answer the phone." Adam rolled his eyes and unlocked the door.

"Yeah, yeah. Question stands." Aaron's voice was strained.

"No. He didn't want to look. Francesca came home."

"What? When?"

"Twenty minutes ago?" Adam outlined the basics of what she'd said and how he left them. "So...maybe the crisis has passed."

Aaron's heavy sigh crackled in his ear. "I hope so. Though there's a lot of work to do to repair...everything. Carol spent some time last night putting together a list of marriage counselors, just in case."

"You really think they need that? Nothing happened."

"That's true. But something just as easily could have happened. Marriage counseling isn't a dirty word, you know. It can be a positive thing. A helpful one. Carol and I have gone a few times over the years when we kept bumping up against a problem we weren't able to resolve on our own."

Adam's eyebrows shot up. "I...had no idea."

"Yeah, well, it doesn't feel all that great at the time to talk about. There's that stigma, you know? Like only people on the verge of divorce go to marriage counseling. It can be a healthy thing though." Aaron cleared his throat. "Thanks for letting us know. I guess I'll give them a little bit and see if they want us to bring the kids by tonight or go ahead and take them to school in the morning. You get the Jordan proposal in your email?"

"Got it. Haven't spent much time looking at it."

"If you could bump that to the top of your list for tomorrow, I'd appreciate it. I think we're going to be better off if we assume Ash'll need a few weeks off to get things in order. I'll try to take the bulk of it, I know you're finishing up at the mission downtown and that's a lot of fiddly, hands-on work. But..."

"I got it. Send me what you need. I'll figure out a way to make it happen." Adam ended the call and shifted into drive. Looked like his afternoon was taking on a considerably different shape than he'd imagined. Hopefully he'd still get a chance to talk to Sara.

20

Sara sank onto the cot and sighed. The room she shared with the three other women on the mission trip was empty, and the quiet was bliss. They'd been here almost a week, and had been running since the plane touched down at the airport. This afternoon, she'd been scheduled to watch kids while the optometrist on the team had clinic hours, but no one had come and after the first hour, he'd sent her back to the church. His wife, who was also his front office staff, was along on the trip, and she'd been happy to watch kids if any showed up.

Sara hadn't waited for them to change their minds.

She didn't consider herself an introvert. In fact, talking to all the different people she met in the course of a typical day of physical therapy was something she considered a perk of the job. For some reason, doing that same work away from home was more exhausting.

Her phone buzzed and she pushed her cot closer to the wall. That way she could keep her cell plugged in while she checked it. She hadn't had an actual conversation with Adam since she'd been gone. They'd texted, but it wasn't the same. She missed hearing his voice.

She pressed the icon that looked like a video camera and waited. Would he have time?

His face appeared on the screen and she sighed, smiling. "Hey, you."

"I didn't know we could do this. It's really good to see your face. I miss you."

"Right there with you. Just one more week though."

"How is it? Are you having fun?"

Fun? Sara wouldn't call it that, necessarily. "It's hot. But it's also fulfilling. The people are so appreciative. And it's nice to know

I'm making a difference, even if all I'm doing is watching kids so their parents can see a doctor."

Adam frowned. "You're watching kids?"

"There hasn't been as much need for what I can do as they thought, initially. So, yeah, I've been doing a lot of childcare and other background support." It was still useful. Everyone appreciated it. Maybe it wasn't what she'd thought she'd be doing, but part of any work like this was learning to roll with what came. Or so they'd said in the planning meetings.

"I'm sorry. I know that's not what you planned."

Sara shrugged. "I'm still helping. And it's better than being in the office while they train the new hires. They weren't excited about letting me take the time off, but they couldn't really stop me since I had the time accrued. How's everything there? How's your brother?"

"They met with Pastor Brown on Wednesday, I think? I'm kind of trying to stay out of it but be available, if that makes sense?"

"You don't want to be in the middle of it."

He shook his head. "I really don't. I mean, if they need me to be, then sure, I'll do whatever I can, but...Sunday was so awkward."

He'd sent several long text messages on Sunday evening filling her in on the afternoon. Awkward was an understatement. She probably would've just walked out, regardless of what they said. On the flip side, there's no way she would've wanted—or even tolerated—having someone else in the room for a conversation like that. "Yeah. I hear you. How's the mission building?"

Adam grinned. "It's going very well. We're almost down to punch out work—the last little details that have to be done before getting the final inspection and occupancy. I figure end of next week we should be ready to schedule that walk through."

"That's great." She cast around for another topic of conversation. She wasn't ready to end the call, but she couldn't keep him on the phone talking about nothing. He surely still had work he should be doing, and the ladies of the church would be here soon to start dinner. She should go help with that since her hands were free. "I guess I should let you go?"

"I don't want you to. But probably. I love you, Sara."

She grinned, the words leaving her warm all over. "Love you, too. I'll text you tomorrow."

"Sounds good. One more week."

"Can't wait." She ended the video chat and stretched. She should go to the kitchen so she was ready to help. Sara tucked her phone under her pillow, leaving it connected to the charger, and slipped her feet into her flip-flops.

The church hallway was empty, but there were voices coming from the main room. Was the rest of the team back already? She'd hoped to make some more friends as part of this trip, but so far that hadn't happened. She couldn't say why and spent too much time late at night running through the possible reasons. Still, she could try. She aimed toward the voices, stopping in her tracks in the doorway.

Luc.

But it couldn't be. He was in Martinique. Where he lived with his wife. Heat flashed across her cheeks. He'd duped her so easily with his smooth ways and his apparent heart for God. He'd worked for the same mission organization Ben did. Thankfully, once his behavior was made public, they'd fired him. Sara pushed away the memories. She wasn't the same woman anymore and, besides, there was no reason he'd be here. It was just another tall, good-looking man with an island accent.

Sara took a deep breath to calm the hammering of her heart and stepped into the room.

Pastor Lonzo looked up and smiled. "Ah, Sara. I think you're the first of the team who's back, though the others should be here soon. Was it a good day?"

She nodded.

"Fantastic. Let me introduce you to Luc Duval. He's a traveling missionary here in the Caribbean, based out of Martinique."

Her mouth went dry, and she worked to school her expression into what she hoped was something bland and noncommittal as Luc turned.

His eyebrows lifted in obvious surprise. "Hello, Sara."

"Luc." She nodded and turned to smile at the pastor. "We've met, in fact."

"Oh?" The pastor turned to Luc. "You were doing mission work in the US?"

How would he get out of the truth? No doubt with charm and arrogance. That seemed to be his usual method. Sara sent up a quick prayer for patience and let go of her anger. Again.

"I used to work for an organization that does international work building wells, that sort of thing, until I felt God calling me to more local, hands-on ministry."

Sara couldn't stop the snort, but tried to cover it with a feigned cough. "It's dusty in here. I hope you'll excuse me. I'm going to go see if the ladies in the kitchen need any help starting supper."

"Oh, but surely you're not on duty tonight? You helped yesterday. And the day before." The pastor frowned. "Isn't there a rotation?"

"I like to do it."

"It's good to see you again, Sara." Luc held out his hand.

Sara arched an eyebrow and nodded to the pastor before heading to the kitchen. Luc Duval. It was bad enough that she was here and essentially useless for anything other than babysitting. What had she done to deserve having to deal with Luc? Mission work? She shook her head, that seemed so incredibly unlikely. Why was he really here?

"Why are you not out on the beach enjoying all that Jamaica has to offer? It doesn't seem right that you'd deprive everyone of seeing you in a bikini." Luc's teeth gleamed white in the sun as he gave Sara a knowing grin.

Ugh. How had she ever fallen for his lines? Snake oil practically dripped off him. He should be selling used cars, not hitting up struggling churches for money they didn't have. She ignored his question and continued wrapping an elastic bandage around the young girl's ankle. "There you are. That should help it feel better. You saw how I wrapped it?"

The girl nodded.

"Good. Keep it wrapped for a week, if you can. Then you should be good as new. And next time, be sure to avoid holes in the sand when you're running after that soccer ball." Sara winked at the girl. "Tell the others I'll be out in just a moment. I think we could all use a snack."

The girl's eyes lit up and she jumped to her feet. She winced as her injured foot came down, tested it, and limped quickly through the open doors that led to the grassy area to the side of the church where kids were kicking a ball.

Sara gathered her first aid kit and stood.

Luc grabbed her arm. "Sara?"

"Don't touch me." Sara jerked her arm away and glared at the man she'd once believed she loved. "What would your wife think?"

"Ah, she understands how it is. A man who is not always at home?" He shrugged and spread his hands. "Fidelity is not reasonable."

That poor woman. Sara shook her head. Not her problem. And she wasn't going to try and make it hers, either. "It is in my book. Now if you'll excuse me, I have work to be doing."

"Ah yes. Babysitting. They are all old enough to care for themselves. Why do you waste your time? Come with me. We can go to a secluded spot I know, perhaps rent a boat?"

"Not interested. Not now. Not ever." She could feel his eyes on her back as she strode out to where the kids played. She wasn't going to give him the satisfaction of turning around though. Hopefully he'd leave soon and she could forget this ever happened.

The afternoon with the kids dragged. There was only so much ball kicking that she could handle. Her attempts to switch the game to something—anything—else had failed miserably. She waved goodbye as the last of the kids headed out into the neighborhood, presumably toward home. She wanted cold water and a chance to put her feet up. At least tomorrow was Sunday. They'd go to services in the morning and then have a blissful afternoon with nothing scheduled. Maybe she could sneak in another video chat with Adam.

Adam.

Should she tell him about Luc? No. There was no reason to, surely. Adam knew all about her previous relationship with the man, and that it was completely over. Hopefully, Luc would be on his way soon. She didn't really understand why he was still here a day later. But that was the pastor's problem, and she wasn't getting involved. There was no point in giving Luc a reason to bring up the past and paint it in whatever ridiculous light he'd choose. Best case, she'd be accused of gossiping, something she'd already seen the pastor take several local women to task for. Worst case? He wouldn't believe her. Best, all things considered, to ignore it.

Sara scooped ice into a cup in the kitchen and filled it with water. She drank it slowly, savoring the cool as it worked its way down her throat.

"Hey." One of the women from the mission team came through the swinging door, her face red and covered with sweat. "Is there ice?"

"Yeah. I'll get you some. You look beat. What were you doing?" Sara grabbed another cup and filled it with ice and water before passing it over.

"Clinic hours. But the little..." she glanced around and lowered her voice, "shack. It was a shack. I have better housing for my garden tools. Anyway, it was hot. No windows, to speak of, just four plywood walls, a floor, and a roof. The doorway was open, because there was no door. And I got the impression that it's someone's home. It was like sitting in an oven all day."

Sara winced. Maybe playing outside with the kids, where she could catch a breeze now and then, wasn't so bad. "Yikes."

"Basically. But the people are so appreciative, it's hard to mind. And they need us." The woman downed the water and reached for the pitcher to refill the cup. "I heard you had a little trouble?"

"Just a twisted ankle. She'll be fine."

The woman frowned. "I hadn't heard about that. Some guy was pestering you?"

Sara sighed. "That was nothing. I met him a year ago, when he worked for a different organization."

"Yeah? He's a nice looking man."

Sara shrugged. It was true enough, but the nice outer packaging hid a slimy interior. "Aren't you married?"

"I am. But you aren't. If the situation was reversed, I'd be taking a second look." The woman drained her cup a second time and set it on the counter. "Just saying."

"I'm seeing someone."

"Ah."

Sara forced a smile and set her own cup in the trash. "I'm going to go rest before dinner. If they need an extra hand when they get here, would you let me know?"

"Of course."

Sara hurried out of the kitchen and down the hall to the room where the women slept. She didn't need anyone trying to match her up with Luc. Or even talk to him again. Where had she heard about his clumsy attempts at flirting? And why wouldn't the man just go away and leave her in peace?

There was nothing for her to do. Sara sighed and looked around the empty church. Several of the doctors were having clinic hours in the area, but they all had spouses traveling with them who were happy to watch any kids who needed minding. The orthopedic specialist was heading home today, having gotten a call during church yesterday that the other doctor in her practice had broken his leg. She had to be there for appointments. But without the orthopedic doc, Sara wasn't likely to get any more PT work. She'd already worked with everyone who said they had general aches and pains. Or at least she'd worked with everyone who was willing to admit it. Maybe she should go home, too.

"Sara." Pastor Lonzo smiled as he hovered in the doorway. "Could you come to my office for a few minutes?"

"Sure." She cast her thoughts around for what this could possibly be about and came up empty. Maybe he realized she was useless and was going to order her home. Or give her something to do around the church. That would be fine. She nodded to the secretary as she followed in the pastor's wake. His office, like the rest of the church, was sparsely decorated. Though his space, at least, had a feeling of permanence. The room was only his office, not a multi-use space like everywhere else in the building save the kitchen and bathrooms.

"Have a seat." He closed the door and moved around his desk. There was an enormous window in the door and his secretary had turned to watch the goings on.

Sara sat in the only other chair and folded her hands in her lap as her stomach clenched. Something about the pastor's demeanor suggested this wasn't going to be pleasant.

He cleared his throat. "I understand you know Mr. Duval? Luc?"

How much should she say? "I think I mentioned that. Yes."

"You were in a relationship with him, though, yes?"

"I thought I was."

The pastor frowned. "I don't understand. What do you mean?"

"Relationship, to me at least, suggests that it's only the two of us. From what I discovered later, that was never the case. So I don't consider the time I dated him anything more than a colossal mistake at the hands of a serial cheater." She squeezed her hands together tighter and fought back the urge to scream. Luc had misused her.

Abused her trust. In some ways, she was grateful though. The disaster of their "relationship" had led her back to Jesus. All the way back instead of the when it suited her compromise that she—and so many others in the modern American church—had been embracing. "He's not trustworthy."

"He said you might try to smear his reputation. He said I could call his wife, should I need to."

Unbelievable. Sara swallowed, trying to rid her mouth of the desert that formed in it. "Did you?"

"Not yet. I wanted to see what you'd say. I have a hard time believing that you would smear the reputation of one of God's missionaries."

"I have someone else you can call, if you're interested in checking stories." Heat seared her cheeks and her hands began to shake. How *dare* Luc do this to her! She'd left him alone. Hadn't said anything about his little mission scam—and that weighed on her conscience. She reached into her pocket for her phone, nearly dropping it on the concrete floor. "His name is Ben Taylor. He works for an international aid organization. The same one Luc previously worked for. I think, if you asked about me and Luc, you'd get a different story from them."

"All they said when I checked his references was that he had worked for them. They wouldn't say anything about the situation surrounding his departure."

Of course they wouldn't. Even someone like Luc got privacy. Surely, Ben would give him the straight story. "Ben's not in H.R. And you're not asking about his work, so much as my relationship with the man. That's all you wanted to know about from me."

The pastor studied her a moment before nodding. "Call him."

Sara took a deep breath and dialed. She put the phone on speaker and set it on the pastor's desk as it rang.

"Sara? This is a nice surprise, but Rebecca's not with me. I had to go into the office today."

"Hi, Ben. I actually needed to talk to you, not Bec. Um. You remember Luc, right?"

"That slime." Ben's breath crackled in the phone's speaker. "I still feel responsible, somewhat, for how he treated you."

"Don't. I'm an adult. My mistakes are my own." And she was never going to make that same mistake again. Even if the temptation was there. Adam...oh, he was temptation to be sure. But they already had a stronger relationship than she'd had in the past because it was built on a friendship. And because they kept their physical attraction on a tight leash.

"Why bring up Luc?"

"He's here."

"He's where? In Jamaica? What's he doing there?"

"Ostensibly raising funds for his mission work in the islands."

Ben snorted. "That's rich. Please tell me no one's falling for it. Did he bring his wife?"

"No. He's alone. He hit on me Saturday, trying to rekindle things."

The pastor's eyes popped.

Sara added in a hurry, "Please don't tell anyone. I handled it."

"Are you sure? Rebecca'd love to fly down there and do him bodily harm for how he treated you last year." Ben's voice was hard.

"I'm sure. But, um, that's why I'm calling. He apparently went to the pastor to try and discredit me first, in case I was thinking of saying something that would jeopardize his fundraising here. I was hoping you might..."

"Put the pastor on the phone."

Relief washed over her and she closed her eyes. "Thank you. He's here."

Sara gestured for the pastor to speak and stood. She turned her back on the desk and let her gaze roam over the single shelf of books on the wall, tuning out their conversation. Her stomach was already roiling, she didn't need to hear any more. How many Christian living books did people read once and then ignore? Maybe she could organize a collection when she returned home. She'd have to ask if that would be useful when he was off the phone.

"I see. Thank you. Here's Sara." The pastor sounded defeated.

Sara turned.

"That all you need, Sara?"

"Yeah, thanks, Ben. Tell Rebecca I miss her. I'll be home Saturday. Maybe sooner."

"I'll let her know. Stay away from Luc. I'm not happy he turned up while you're down there."

"It's a coincidence, I'm sure."

Ben grunted. "Maybe. Call if you need anything else."

"Thanks. I will. Bye." Sara pressed end and looked at the pastor. He was slumped at his desk, his head in his hands.

He gestured for her to sit. "I'm sorry."

Sara nodded. "Me too."

"I felt something was off. But his explanation...was plausible and would have taken care of my misgivings. I am sorry for the harm he did to you and for my own part in re-opening that wound."

She nodded. Had the wound re-opened? Had it ever completely closed? She didn't trust people—men in particular—very easily anymore. Look at Adam. She loved him, but still shrank away from fully trusting him. What did that say about her?

The pastor smiled. "You're very quiet. Can I pray for you?"

"Of course." She bowed her head. The pastor's words were soothing and eased something in her heart. When he ended the prayer, she looked up. "Thank you."

"It is my pleasure. You said you might be leaving before the end of the week? Not because of this, I hope?"

"No. There's nothing for me to do, and I hate feeling like I'm dead weight."

"Hmm. There must surely be something you can do?"

Sara shrugged. "Not according to the team."

21

Adam stood at the baggage claim and scanned the crowd. She should be here. Where was she? Two weeks wasn't that long, in the overall scheme of things, but he'd missed her. Was that...there she was. He raised his hand above his head and waved. Sara's gaze passed right over him. He frowned. She looked tired and upset. This last week had been hard—boring, she'd said—but shouldn't she be glad to be home?

He shouldered his way through the clumps of people. "Sara!"

She turned, her lips curving up, but the smile didn't reach her eyes. "Hi."

"Hi yourself." He held out the bouquet of mixed blooms. "It's good to see you."

"Thanks. These are lovely. And they smell good. You didn't have to come get me though, I could've taken a cab."

Adam wrapped his arms around her. Sara stiffened slightly before relaxing and letting her head drop to his shoulder. "I missed you. Besides, a taxi would cost a mint. Let's get your bag."

"Okay." Sara stepped back and threaded her fingers through his. "Did you get the final inspection at the mission like you were hoping?"

Adam grinned. "We did. Passed with flying colors. Jerry said they were going to spend the weekend getting furniture and decorations handled and start moving people in next week. I guess he already started the application process. I know they'll be at capacity sooner than he wants, so he's trying to get, and stay, ahead of it."

"That's outstanding. Congratulations." Sara pulled her phone out of her pocket, frowned and tapped at it before shoving it back into her pocket.

"Everything okay?" She was acting odd. "What did you end up doing for your last week?"

"I'm just tired. Um." Sara watched the bags circle on the conveyor. "A little bit of this and that. I painted a room in the church that they decided needed freshening. I helped put together some rain barrels that they pass out to the community to help everyone have clean water. They'd talked about doing some abstinence education, but that fell through. I can't say I minded that. I spent some time sitting and talking with the women of the church. Once they realized I didn't have anything to do, they kept showing up with their Bibles. We'd study and pray. But it was clear they were just there to keep me occupied. Oh, that's it."

Adam followed her pointing finger and grabbed the bag off the belt, narrowly avoiding taking out an older man who reached for the suitcase behind Sara's. "This one?"

She nodded.

"Okay. Shall we?"

"Definitely. I want a shower. And a nap."

Adam chuckled. "All I wanted when we got back in January was a long, hot shower. You had actual facilities though, right?"

"Yeah. But it's still not like showering at home. Since there were only seven of us, we didn't completely use up the water heater, but it was close. Especially if someone ended up needing to shower again, off schedule. You know what? Maybe I'll even take a bath. I'm not usually one for baths, but I might make an exception."

Adam struggled to keep from picturing her submerged to her chin in steaming water. His mouth went dry, and he hauled his thoughts back to the present as they dashed across a crosswalk to the short-term parking. "Think you'll want to go to church tomorrow?"

"Would you mind if I begged off?"

His heart sank. After two weeks of the singles class, he'd been looking forward to going back to Kevin and Lydia's class. Or trying something new. There was nothing stopping him from doing that still, but without Sara, he probably wouldn't. "Molly was telling me about another class they tried. It's a mixed bag of singles and couples of all ages. I was thinking we might give it a shot."

"Next week?"

Adam noted the shadows under her eyes and nodded. She was clearly exhausted. There was no need to push. He clicked the unlock button for his truck and opened the rear passenger door, hefting her suitcase inside. "Want to put your carryon back here, too?"

Sara dropped her backpack in and wrenched open the front door. "I really do appreciate you picking me up."

"It's my pleasure." He caught the door as she was starting to close it and leaned in, brushing his lips across hers.

"Adam..."

"Yeah?"

She licked her lips and shook her head. "Nothing. Never mind."

He studied her a moment before nodding and closing her door. There was something going on, but she didn't want to talk about it. Obviously. He could be patient.

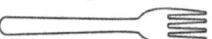

"You're right, this is a good class. Maybe I'll see if Sara wants to try it next week." Adam walked beside Molly and Karl as they headed to the parking lot after church. "Although, Kevin and Lydia's class is great, too."

"There are a lot of good options once you break out of the age-normed one. I'm struggling to understand why I stayed in the singles class as long as I did." Molly wrinkled her nose. "Maybe because my best friend was there."

Adam chuckled. "Yeah, well, you kept me there, too. So we're even. They should do a seminar on how you know it's time to leave."

"Seminar? How about intervention?" Karl grinned. "I only stuck around for Molly, myself. Imagine if one of us had been brave enough to leave sooner."

"Yeah, well there's no going back now. Have you heard the latest Jessica is spinning?" Molly pulled a face. "She needs to get a life. She clearly has too much time on her hands."

Adam stopped by his truck and sighed. "What is it now?"

Karl nudged Molly with his elbow and shook his head.

"I think he deserves to know." Molly frowned.

"It's just gossip. She has no facts. You know this." Karl looked at Adam. "Ignore it. Ignore Jessica."

He wanted to know. Then he could confront her and...what? It wouldn't change anything. In fact, it was liable to make it worse. Maybe Karl was right. "You know what? Just leave it. I'll either hear it eventually or she'll move on to something else unfounded. Gossip isn't good for any of us."

Molly nodded, her expression betraying her reluctance. "If you're sure."

"I am. But thanks. I know you've got my back." Adam patted her shoulder. "Now, I'm going to head across the street and pick up the Chinese food I ordered online before I left for church and see if Sara's feeling up to lunch."

Karl shook his head. "Risky move. What if she's still sleeping?"

"Then you and I have Chinese in the fridge for later this week. I don't see a downside. You two have fun." Adam pulled open his truck's door and climbed in. The reality was that he wasn't as sure of himself as he was trying to sound. There was a very real possibility that Sara would ignore his knocking. Or open it, take the food, and push him away. But he wanted to see her. *Needed* to hold her, even if only for a minute. He wasn't going to dwell on the fact that it didn't seem like she'd missed him at all.

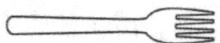

Wednesday morning, Adam parked his truck at the curb in front of Asher's house and sipped from his travel mug. It was unusual, though not unheard of, to have a mid-week in-person meeting. Usually they just had a three-way call and went about their business. Something must be up.

Aaron pulled up behind him and beeped his horn.

Adam pushed open his door, grabbed his phone and coffee, and strode toward his brother's truck. "Morning."

"I got donuts. Figured we might as well, since we were actually in one place." Aaron lifted the box off his passenger seat and hopped out of his truck. "Ready?"

"Sure. Do I get a hint about the meeting topic at all?"

Aaron shook his head. "If I knew, I'd tell you. Ash is the one who called it."

Something to do with him and Francesca then? But how did that impact the business? He wouldn't sell out, would he? It wasn't like they didn't need to have an income. No. Adam pushed that thought away. That couldn't be it.

Aaron grabbed the doorknob and twisted it, stepping into the house as he called out, "We're here."

"In the kitchen." Asher's voice echoed out to greet them.

Adam closed the door and followed Aaron back. It didn't feel like the same house he'd been in just a couple of weeks ago. The sense of gloom and doom that had permeated the air when Francesca'd left was gone. That had to be a good sign. Didn't it?

Aaron dropped the donuts on the island and slid onto a stool before flipping open the box. "So?"

Asher reached in and snagged a chocolate glazed. He took a bite without saying anything.

Adam shook his head and reached for a filled donut that had a little bit of red jam oozing from it. He bit in and smiled. Raspberry. Maybe his brother loved him after all. "I'm with Aaron. So?"

Asher chuckled. "It's nothing bad. I mostly wanted to say thank you for giving me—us—some space. We're not back to where we should be, but we're on the right path, and I think I'm ready to pick up the reins again and do my job."

"He's more than ready. Please get him out of the house," Francesca called from the dining room.

Aaron laughed and raised his voice, "I brought donuts. You can have one if you come in and say hi."

Francesca padded into the room, still in her pajamas, her hair twisted into a messy bun. Her cheeks flamed red. "I'm so sorry. I know this hurt both of you as well as my family."

"We are your family." Adam reached for her hand and squeezed it.

"I know. I...it's so humiliating. Can you possibly forgive me?"

Aaron nudged the box of treats toward her. "Already done."

Francesca's eyes filled and she reached into the box, drawing out a plain donut. She set it on a napkin before moving to stand beside Asher and wrap her arms around him. She laid her head on his shoulder, keeping her gaze on Adam and Aaron. "We're going to get through this and come out on the other side stronger for it."

Asher kissed the top of her head. "With God's help, we absolutely are."

"I'll let you get back to your meeting. Thanks for the donut and...for everything." She slipped out of the room.

Asher watched her leave, a smile on his lips. He turned back to his brothers. "So. I'd like to come back. I do want to keep to business hours though. Right now, I can't afford to get back into the trap of putting work before Fran and the kids."

"None of us should get into that trap." Adam reached for another donut. "Seriously. If we're all that busy constantly, then we either need to turn down work or hire some help. I haven't been putting in those kinds of hours. Have you, Aaron?"

Aaron shook his head. "I did for a bit, when we were just starting out, but Carol straightened me out fairly fast. Leave work at the office, man. No one will fault you for that."

"Okay." Asher rubbed the back of his neck. "I guess I haven't wanted to let you two down."

Adam snorted. "Next time you make a joke, warn me so I don't almost snarf my coffee."

"What he said." Aaron pointed to Adam. "Seriously. You can't let us down unless you get so busy working that your life falls apart. Then you not only let us down, but you let yourself down as well."

"All right. You're right. You might need to remind me. Some habits die hard." Asher pulled the donut box closer and looked at the contents. "Now, tell me what projects I'm getting back and where they are. Catch me up."

22

"Let me hold her." Sara held out her arms for the baby.

Rebecca handed her over and collapsed onto Sara's couch. "Is Jen coming?"

"Supposed to be. She was amazed I was skipping prayer meeting, so she figured she could skip whatever show it is that has her glued to her TV on Wednesday nights lately. I still don't understand why she doesn't at least DVR things so she can skip the commercials." Sara kissed the baby's head and made a face, laughing when she was rewarded with a smile. "You didn't tell me she was smiling."

"Oh, yeah. She's almost six months now—we're nearly at the end of May, you realize. She's smiling, rolling over, sitting up...all kinds of fun tricks." Rebecca yawned. "Except sleeping through the night. She hasn't mastered that one yet."

"You love it." Her friend might try to sound like she was complaining, but it was clear from her voice that she wouldn't go back for the world.

"I really do. When we got pregnant so fast after we got married, I was worried. I mean, I'd always thought we'd have a couple of years just us, you know? But now? It's wonderful. I can't think why I wanted to wait." Rebecca dug in the bag at her feet and extracted a burp cloth. "Here. You need this. She's also teething. Drool everywhere."

Sara blotted the dribbles of drool on Chloe's chin and kissed the tip of her nose. "Let's go see if that's Auntie Jen knocking at the door, shall we?"

"I can take her back."

"She's no problem." Sara stood and cradled the baby close. She grinned and opened the door. "It *is* auntie Jen."

Jen grunted. "You're awfully chipper."

Sara frowned and closed the door. "What's the matter with you?"

"Just...work. I've got a big deadline coming up and two people on my team are underperforming, and they may end up getting let go. I think they're going to make me do it. I've never fired someone. I don't want to fire someone. I don't even know how you do that. It's...horrible. Even the thought is horrific. And David's no help. His advice was to just do it. Like I'm a basketball shoe." Jen huffed out a breath. "So I might've picked a fight with him, and now he's annoyed with me. I'm too embarrassed and mad to do anything about it. I knew marriage was going to be hard sometimes, but I don't think I realized just how hard."

"Here, hold the baby." Sara passed the burp cloth and Chloe to Jen. "You can't stay upset when you're holding a baby."

"Yes, you can." Rebecca raised her hand. "When you're coming up on six months of no sleep, you can hold a baby and be upset."

"Okay, okay, fine. Under those conditions. But in these, I think it'll be soothing." Sara chuckled and shook her head. "But you have to hold her like she's a person, not a bomb that's about to go off."

Jen brought the baby closer and sniffed her head. "Oohhh. That smell. Why do babies smell so good?"

"Mystery of the ages."

Rebecca laughed. "Not a mystery. It's called baby shampoo. You can smell like it too for the low price of five bucks."

"Sleep deprivation has killed your soul." Sara frowned at Rebecca before turning to Jen. "Isn't that better?"

"It is. Can I take her to work with me? She can help me fire the two guys on my team."

"I think I'm going to pass on letting my daughter be an ax man this early in her career, thanks all the same." Rebecca rolled her eyes. "Now, tell us all about Jamaica, Sara."

Sara's phone buzzed and her stomach clenched. Not again. Her hand trembled as she reached to tap the screen and open the text. The image of Luc in a skimpy swimsuit filled the screen and she quickly tapped delete. The phone buzzed again. This time she hit the power button.

"What's that about?" Jen nodded toward Sara's phone.

Sara swallowed and the whole story of Luc's arrival in Jamaica, his attempts to flirt, the confrontation with the pastor, and the unpleasantness from Luc after the pastor sent him on his way came spilling out. "After he left, he started trying to chat with me on social media. I blocked him. Then he started texting. I'd block him and he'd move to another number. Now he's moved on from flirtatious, suggestive texts to photos. At least in this one he had on a swimsuit. He hasn't always. I don't know what to do."

"What did Adam say?" Jen jiggled the baby as she began to whimper.

"Are you insane? I haven't told him. He can't know—you have to promise."

"Why? You didn't ask for this, you haven't done anything wrong. Don't you think he deserves to know someone's harassing his girlfriend?" Rebecca leaned forward and dug a bottle out of her diaper bag, offering it to Jen.

Maybe Adam deserved to know. She couldn't say for certain one way or the other. But... "It's not like he can do anything about it. It's just going to make him mad. And...what if he thinks I'm encouraging it?"

"I think you're underestimating him." Jen popped the top off the bottle and tipped it into the baby's mouth. "Don't you trust him to know you by now?"

Trust. It kept coming down to trust. She'd trusted Luc. Look how that had turned out. She'd trusted herself, at one point, to stay faithful to God until she was married. That had turned out just as poorly. Adam knew about her past. Would he really believe she wasn't doing anything wrong? Her voice came out as a whisper. "I don't know."

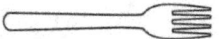

It was as if an entire busy anthill had taken up residence in her stomach. Deep breathing wasn't helping, either. It was a date. Just a date. With Adam. She'd been on dates with him before. She'd stayed in for dates with him. They'd kissed. Granted, she'd kept that to a minimum and as tame as she could manage—not an easy feat by any stretch of the imagination—but it was easy to want, easy to let chemistry drive the train. There was more to their relationship than chemistry though.

They had friendship. They shared a deep love for Jesus.

And trust?

Sara took another deep breath and let it out slowly. She trusted Adam. She had a harder time trusting herself.

The cheerful tappity-tap on her door made her jolt. Sara smoothed the skirt of her dress as she crossed to answer. There was no need for nerves. They were past that.

"Hi."

Adam's eyebrows lifted as his gaze roamed over her. "Wow. You look amazing. Am I under dressed?"

"You always look great." Heat spread across her cheeks. She probably looked like a tomato. "I mean..."

Adam put a finger to her lips, grinning. "I don't mind if you stop there. The feeling's mutual. You ready?"

"Yeah." Sara grabbed the little evening purse she'd switched to and hooked the strap over her shoulder after checking to ensure her keys were inside. "Where are we headed?"

"You like Peruvian chicken?"

She nodded.

"Cool. I was thinking we'd do that before the movie."

"Perfect." She slipped her hand in his, her chest loosening as his fingers curled around hers and squeezed. "How was prayer meeting?"

"Good. As usual. I'm glad you're feeling better."

"I wasn't sick...just still tired and getting back into the routine at work—going from a week of basically nothing in Jamaica to the insanity of understaffed and overbooked threw me."

"I get it."

She glanced at him. Was he telling the truth?

His eyes locked with hers and one corner of his mouth poked up. "I really do. When we got back in January, I thought I'd need a week off to recover. It's okay. I just missed you."

"I missed you, too. I love you, Adam."

He grinned. "I love you, too."

The drive was quiet, marked only by occasional snippets of conversation and the low hum of the Christian radio station, but it wasn't awkward. It was settled. Cozy. Comfortable. They parked near the restaurant at the strip mall and walked hand-in-hand between the cars.

After they'd ordered, Adam cleared his throat. "You remember I told you about my brother Asher?"

"Sure. How are they doing?"

"Wednesday we had a little status meeting at his house. It sounds like they're doing pretty well. Lots of counseling and healing still in the future, but they're making a good start. He's coming back to work, which'll be nice. I like being busy, but even sharing the workload with Aaron it's been crazier than I anticipated. That was nice while you were away, but now that you're home, I'm kind of looking forward to spending as much time with you as I can swing."

Her heart lifted. When had anyone she'd dated actually enjoyed time with her and said so? Never. Sure, she'd hung out with guys, gone on dates, but it was clear from the beginning that they were biding their time for the minimum acceptable waiting period before they could be physical. And once sex was on the table, there'd been very little pretense of being together for anything else. It was...shallow. Hollow. How had she not realized that before? Her phone chimed. Sara's heart raced, but she ignored it. "I'm good with that."

"Do you need to check that? It's okay. I know you probably have lots of catching up to do with Rebecca and Jen."

She laughed. "Not really. I texted them while I was gone, too. And they came over Wednesday night."

Hurt flashed across Adam's features. "I see."

"I..." Sara closed her eyes. Now she'd put her foot in it. "I needed to see them."

"Sure. I get it. It's okay."

He wouldn't meet her gaze. What was she supposed to do? Her phone chimed again and she reached into her purse to turn it off. "Adam...I'm sorry. I was tired."

"Don't worry about it, okay? It's not like you had to miss me as much as I missed you. There aren't rules for this kind of thing. I guess...I guess I thought we were on the same page though."

"We are." Sara's heart hammered. She couldn't bear the thought of losing him. "Please believe me."

He stared over her head for what felt like an eternity before nodding. "I'll try. Good to catch up with them, I imagine."

Sara hunched her shoulders. "Yeah. Jen's stressed about having to fire two of the people on her team. Rebecca brought the baby, so I got some snuggles. She's so happy...if I didn't love her, I think I'd despise her."

Adam offered a tiny smile. "My brothers are like that sometimes. Even with Francesca's situation, she and Asher are like the cover models for a marriage magazine. Aaron and Carol are worse. I want that."

Sara couldn't have looked away if she wanted to. For the first time in her adult life, she allowed a sliver of hope to take root in her heart. This was a man who'd love her, faults and all. He listened to her and enjoyed her company, not just her body. She loved him. Real love, like the Bible described. She had no doubt that if she did the corny test her mother used to harp about and put Adam's name instead of the word "love" into First Corinthians thirteen, he'd pass with flying colors. "So do I."

"What is so important that you had to drag me out of Sunday school and into the ladies room?" Jen crossed her arms and leaned against the stall by the sinks.

Sara peered under the stalls to make sure they were alone. "I'm in love with Adam."

"Didn't we already know this? You've been saying 'I love you' for weeks."

"I know. But I mean I'm really in love. Capital L. He's the one. And I think, maybe, he's thinking marriage too." Sara pressed a hand to her stomach. "Is it supposed to make me want to vomit?"

Jen chuckled. "A little, yeah. Congratulations. Did you tell him about Luc?"

"No. Are you insane? I'm not trying to scare him away. I'm trying to tie my life to his forever. Stalker-ish exs aren't the way to do that."

"You're so wrong about that. You need to tell him. Sooner rather than later. In fact, if I had a time machine and it could only be used once, I'd make you use it to go back and tell Adam about it while you were still in Jamaica. Please reconsider. You're risking everything, you know that, right?"

"How?" Sara held up a hand. "Never mind. Look, I have a solution. I'm going to get a new phone number. I'll tell him I lost my phone."

"So...a lie? That's your brilliant plan? You've lost your mind." Jen shook her head. "When—and I do mean when, not if—this blows up in your face, it's going to be ugly. Don't compound it with a lie."

It wasn't going to blow up, though. Why wouldn't Jen see that? This was the perfect solution. A new number—an *unlisted* one— would make it impossible for Luc to find and harass her. She'd only give the number to her friends and Adam would never have to know about the smarmy photos Luc had taken to sending.

"I still don't understand why you haven't just blocked his number."

"I *did*. He keeps using new ones. I guess pre-paid wireless makes it easy for him to have as many phones as he wants. Or he has some way of spoofing phone numbers. Whatever it is, blocking him hasn't stopped it. I just ignore texts from numbers I don't recognize now. But I still know they're there. It's...creepy. A new number fixes that."

"You need to tell Adam. I'm not backing down from that. Lies are a terrible foundation for a relationship."

Yeah, well, maybe that was true. But the truth, or in this case what would look like the truth even though it really wasn't true, was worse. No way Adam would believe Luc was doing all of this with no provocation. And the derisive responses Luc had sent the few times she'd told him to knock it off...well, those were probably nothing compared to what Adam would say.

No. A new phone was the better plan. She'd go out during lunch tomorrow and take care of it.

23

"Hey." Molly looked up from the game she was playing with Karl and smiled as Adam shut the apartment door. "Have a good afternoon?"

"Really did. We went up to Great Falls and hiked by the river. It was a nice day—I'm surprised the summer heat hasn't started up yet. We stopped for an early dinner on the way home. I tried to stretch it into a movie at her place, but I guess she's still recovering from the mission trip." Adam shrugged and ignored the pang that came with the memory of Sara's rejection. It wasn't a rejection of *him*, just his idea. Or that's what he was going to keep telling himself until it stuck. She'd spent six hours with him after church. It wasn't as if she'd blown him off completely. "What did you two do?"

Molly held up her hand and wiggled her fingers.

Adam frowned. "Huh?"

"Geez, guys are dense. Look close." Molly wiggled her fingers more frantically while Karl started to laugh.

"He's never going to get it. Just tell him." Karl hit a button on his game controller that paused the action on the screen.

Adam shook his head. "You two are crazy."

"We're crazy." Molly sighed and stood. She got close and held her left hand in Adam's face, grinning. "Does this help?"

"That's a pretty...oh. Oh!" Adam laughed and shot a glance at Karl. "Seriously? No head's up?"

"You can't keep a secret."

"Whatever. She's been half in love with you for three years. I never said a word." Adam kissed Molly's cheek. "Congratulations. Though I'm still not sure what you see in him."

"Three years?" Karl's eyes were wide. "Seriously?"

Molly nodded. "Adam's a vault. Speaking of that...?"

"What?" Adam rounded the couch and sat on the end while Molly settled back into her spot.

"If it won't break her confidence, how's Sara doing with the whole Luc thing?"

"Luc thing? Who's Luc? What thing?"

Molly and Karl exchanged a look.

Karl stood. "I'm gonna run out and get some ice cream. Molly was saying we should celebrate our engagement with ice cream. Maybe cake. Cake is always good, right?"

Adam realized his mouth was hanging open and snapped it shut. He cleared his throat and focused on Molly, his lungs burning like he couldn't quite get air in them. "So?"

"I just assumed...I mean...oh man." Molly pinched the bridge of her nose like she always did when she was organizing her thoughts. "I only overheard a little. Jessica was crowing about how she and a couple of others in the group were helping Luc play a practical joke on Sara. I guess he showed up at the church in Jamaica, and Sara was somehow responsible for him getting sent on his way."

"Why would they help him?"

Molly shrugged. "Sara brought him to church with her several times. That was back when she hung out with that crowd...maybe they're all friends? I don't know. Maybe he convinced them to help out with some sob story about how Sara's cost him two jobs now."

"That man...when I think of what he did to her I want to kill him."

Molly nodded. "Yeah, I hear you. Anyway, I guess he figured the easier way to get around Sara would be to hook back up with her. She wasn't having it, though, so he got some of the people in Jessica's group to help him send texts constantly. Jessica was saying how it must be driving her batty to have her phone going off all the time. She seemed to think it was a big joke. But I heard one of the guys saying how he'd been attaching pictures that he'd gotten online to his."

"Pictures? Like...dirty pictures."

"That was my assumption, yeah."

Adam shook his head. Why hadn't she said something? Her phone had been pinging a lot. She'd ignored it and finally just turned it off. In fact, her phone had been off quite a bit since she'd been back. He'd left voicemail more often than not when he tried to call. He'd figured she'd gotten used to being unplugged in Jamaica. But this...why would she keep it from him?

"She didn't say anything." Molly winced.

"No." His eyes burned. Did he matter to her at all? Really matter? "How could she hide something like that?"

"I don't know her well enough to say for sure, but I wonder if she thought she was protecting you somehow."

"Protecting me? I'm supposed to protect her! I love her...I've been trying to decide if it was too soon to propose. Now...what am I supposed to do?"

"I don't know what to tell you. But if it was me, I'd need to talk to her about it."

"Yeah." Adam scrubbed his hands over his face. "That's as good a place to start as any. Tell Karl to save me a slice of cake."

"Adam. Be gentle, okay?"

He nodded, swallowing back a vicious retort. Gentle. It was probably better than throttling her. But it might not be as satisfying.

Adam flexed his hands before knocking on Sara's door. Knocking, not banging. That was a step in the right direction. He wouldn't say he'd cooled off on the drive over, but he'd settled into a low boil. That was something, at least. He knocked again.

"Adam?" Sara pulled open the door, her brows drawn together. "Is something wrong?"

"You tell me."

She blinked and widened the door. "You wanna come in?"

It beat standing in the hall. He nodded and brushed past her, barely noticing that she was in her pajamas and had some kind of pink goo all over her face.

"If you give me a minute, I can go wash this off."

"It's fine." He turned, stuffed his hands in his pockets, and eyed her. "Were you ever going to tell me?"

"Tell you what?" The pink stuff made it harder to read her emotions, but understanding was there in her eyes.

Adam shook his head. He'd planned a whole speech on his way over here, but now? "Really?"

Sara shrugged. "You lost me."

His heart cracked. If that was the way she wanted to play it...that was fine. "I never would've thought you'd lie to me. Obviously, my definition of love is a lot different from yours. I guess I'll see you around. Good bye, Sara."

"Adam..." Anguish hid behind her words.

He turned at the door and waited.

Sara didn't speak.

He swallowed, wrenched open the door, and strode down the hall, his cracked heart shattering into a million tiny pieces.

24

"Come on in. Rebecca's in the kitchen." Ben opened the door wider and stepped back. "You all right?"

Sara shook her head.

Ben patted her shoulder and offered a sympathetic smile. "I'll be upstairs."

Sara glanced around Rebecca's townhouse as she crossed the living room to the kitchen. They hadn't changed much from when Rebecca lived here alone. Little things, here and there, like pictures from their wedding and baby toys on the floor that the cats were batting around.

Rebecca slid a steaming mug across the counter to Sara. Marshmallows bobbed on top.

Sara wrapped her hands around the cocoa but didn't sip. The warmth was nice on her hands.

"So."

Tears fell down Sara's cheeks and she stared into the steaming drink.

Fabric rustled and Rebecca's arm came around her shoulders. "Tell me what happened."

"I told you about Luc last week. He wouldn't give up. Still hasn't, actually. I was going to get a new phone. New number. And just leave it. But Adam found out."

"And he reacted poorly."

Sara nodded, dragging a hand across her cheek. "You could say that. He came over last night and asked—well, hinted around. I didn't want to tell him. I had my plan and it would all just go away...and he basically called me a liar and left. I think he must hate me now. I don't know, though, because he won't answer my texts or calls."

"Oh, Sara." Rebecca sighed. "You know I understand wanting to hide from things, no matter how complicated it makes life, right?"

"Yeah."

"But you saw how badly that worked out for me. Why would you go there?"

"It's not the same. I wasn't changing my name and moving across the country. I was just going to get a new phone number. It's not the same."

"At the core it is. You weren't honest and you tried to hide behind a lie."

Sara sniffled. This...wasn't what she'd hoped for. She needed a friend. Not a beat down. "Okay. Thanks. I know you're busy, so I'll get out of your hair."

"Sara."

"No, it's fine. Have a good night." She slid off the stool and started toward the door, ignoring Rebecca's attempts to get her attention. Maybe Rebecca could call Adam and congratulate him on his narrow escape.

In her car, Sara turned off the radio and watched the lights as she drove. She didn't want to go home. Jen...wasn't any more likely to be sympathetic than Rebecca. Having friends who told you the truth could be good. When it wasn't annoying.

Even if she was wrong—and she wasn't ready to admit that just yet—couldn't Rebecca have patted her on the back and offered to trash Adam? He'd walked away. Just turned and closed the door politely on everything they'd shared. He hadn't even had the emotion to slam it. Maybe their definitions of love were different, because in her mind, loving someone should at least leave you heartbroken when you walked away.

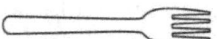

By Friday, Sara's heart was numb. Adam wasn't acknowledging her. He'd been at prayer meeting on Wednesday, but had looked through or around her the entire time and had slipped out the back before she could corner him when it was over.

Jen and Rebecca weren't much better. Neither one was sympathetic to her plight. They were one hundred percent on Adam's side. Most of the gang was getting together at Season's Bounty for dinner and to hang out tonight, but she didn't see the point. They'd either all pile on and tell her how terrible she was to have not told Adam immediately or they'd give her pitying looks. She didn't want either.

Which left her at home, alone, on Friday night.

Welcome to the new normal.

Sara sighed. She'd been here before. She could do it again. Apparently, this was her lot in life.

It was fine. Or it would be. Single wasn't bad. Look at the Apostle Paul. He was single, and God had used him mightily. Maybe there was something big in store for her, some way for God to use her. It wasn't likely to be mission work though. Not after the fiasco in Jamaica. Sure, she'd helped the first week, a little, but after that? She was dead weight, and everyone knew it.

She'd keep praying. Maybe she'd get some insight at some point.

She plopped down on the couch and pulled a throw over her legs. She'd see what was on TV. Maybe she should get a pet. Then, at least, she'd have some companionship. Sara wrinkled her nose. Pets were messy and required a lot of time. Beside all that, she lived in a pet-free building, unless you counted fish. She didn't.

She clicked on the TV and hit the button for the guide. There was a new cheesy sci-fi movie on. Her heart panged. Adam was probably watching it with Molly and Karl. Or just Molly. Maybe now that he'd gotten Sara out of his system, he'd realize he really was in love with Molly and finally make a move. They were perfect for each other. No crazy past to trip anyone up. Just sunshine and buttercups all day, every day.

She deliberately switched to re-runs of a sitcom. Time to try something new. Improbable alien combinations were amusing, but they weren't something the average girl was interested in.

Oh, who was she kidding?

She flipped back to the movie and settled in. Maybe, if she tried very hard, she could keep her thoughts from straying to Adam through the whole movie.

Her phone buzzed.

Sara cringed. It had been two days since she'd gotten anything from an unknown number. Was it too much to expect that he'd finally given up?

Her stomach in knots, she tapped the screen. Jen. Probably pestering her for not showing up at dinner. She set the phone back on the coffee table without reading the message. She'd let Adam down. Her friends had let her down. Really, what was the point?

The phone buzzed again.

Sara powered it down and went back to the movie.

Alone. She could master being alone. It just might take some time.

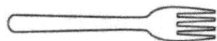

"Where've you been hiding?" Jen cornered Sara as she was hurrying out of the sanctuary.

She sighed. Her plan had been going so well right up to now. "Not hiding. Just busy. You all have your lives, I have mine. You know this."

"Seriously? That's what you're going to go with?" Jen shook her head. "Do you know me at all? I'm the queen of shutting people out. It's not going to work."

Sara managed a faint smile. "It's going to have to. I've gotta run."

Jen matched her steps as Sara headed for the parking lot. When she decided to, Jen could be persistent. And annoying. "Where do you possibly have to go on Sunday morning when you're usually in a small group?"

"Why do you care?" Sara stopped and crossed her arms. "You and Rebecca both made it clear that you're on his side with this. So that's just dandy for you. The three of you—heck, get everyone else involved and make it a party—can hang out and talk about what a loser I am. That's fine. I never tried to hide my past from anyone, and when it tried to sneak back in, I tried to handle it. I don't see what's so wrong with that. I sure didn't get any help from any of you. So you know what? Just leave me alone. You've been doing a pretty good job of that all this week when I thought I needed you. Now that I realize I don't, you can just stay away."

Sara spun and slammed out the doors into the parking lot, her blood boiling. Some friends. Well, she didn't need them. She didn't need anyone. She'd done just fine on her own for the last year, and she could go back to it.

Tears burned the back of her eyes as she unlocked her car and slid behind the wheel. She leaned her head back and stared at the ceiling. Who was she kidding? Not herself, at any rate. Maybe she'd convinced Jen, though—and the rest of the crowd in the lobby. She sighed. It wasn't like this was the first time she'd been fodder for the gossip mill at church. She ought to be used to the humiliation by now. Sara blew her nose and started the car. She had things to do, even if Jen didn't believe her.

Yesterday, after she'd pried herself off the sofa, she'd realized that what she needed was a change. She'd known that for a while—that was why she'd gone to Jamaica in December in the first place. Vacation had helped. Temporarily. But it was time to evaluate. Past time, if she was honest. So she'd done exactly that and come to the realization that a physical therapist could work anywhere. She didn't have to stay in the D.C. area if she didn't want to.

A few hours online had convinced her that there were opportunities to be grabbed. This afternoon was for fixing up her resume and starting down that path. Change. It was past time.

25

"Adam. Wait up."

Adam stopped in the parking lot and turned. He frowned as he saw one of Sara's friends scurrying toward him. This was the fourth week he'd hurried out of prayer meeting before closing to avoid having to talk to anyone. Sara didn't try to talk to him anymore, which made it less awkward. But it didn't ease any of the hurt. Every time he saw her, his heart broke all over again, but he didn't know how to fix it. If she didn't trust him enough to tell the truth...well, they didn't have anything to build on.

"Hi. Thanks. Sorry." The woman blew out a breath and fanned her face. "I don't know if you remember me? I'm Jen."

"Right. Hi. What's up?" Not his most gracious greeting, but he wanted to leave, go home, and bury himself in work. At least that kept his mind off his broken heart. Sort of.

"Did you know Sara's moving?"

His stomach dropped and the edges of his vision grayed. He shook his head and tried to pull the pieces of his scattered thoughts back together. "I hadn't heard that. Where?"

"She isn't sure yet. She has her resume out and has done a handful of phone interviews. She's waiting to hear...but she's planning on submitting her resignation on Friday." Jen's gaze was piercing. "I thought—hoped—you might think it was worth doing something about that."

"What is there to do? She made her decision."

"Did you ask her to explain? I don't agree with what she did, but I do understand why she chose it."

"I asked her about it. She acted like she had no idea what I was talking about. I don't know where to go with that. If she wanted to explain, she had a chance. She didn't take it." Adam tucked his hands in his pockets. "I wasn't worth it to her, I guess. It's not like she's been beating down my door trying to get me to see reason."

Jen frowned. "You're both so stubborn. Let me ask you this. Do you believe she cheated on you with Luc?"

"What? No. He was pestering her, and she didn't think I deserved to know or have a chance to defend her—to support her. She shut me out. But I know she's not that woman anymore. Is that what she thinks?"

"I don't know what she thinks. You're not the only one she shut out. But it's the spin Jessica's spreading around."

Adam made a rude noise. "No one with brains listens to anything Jessica has to say."

Jen smiled. "On that we can agree. One more question, and I'll leave you alone."

"Okay?"

"Do you still love her?"

"I'm trying not to."

"That's not a no."

Adam rubbed his neck. "It's not a no, but it doesn't change anything. She doesn't trust me, and that doesn't work for me."

"Don't you ever get scared and try to hide?"

"That's more than one question. Have a good afternoon." He pulled open the door to his truck.

"Aren't you going to miss her at all?"

Adam paused halfway in the seat. "I already do. Every minute of every day."

He drove on autopilot, his thoughts disjointed, and only realized where he was when he pulled along the curb in front of his brother's house. He turned off the engine and sat in the silence of the truck's cab staring at the lights as they winked off in the kids' bedrooms.

After about twenty minutes, the front door opened and Asher stepped out, crossed the lawn, and tugged open the passenger door. "Here. Since you didn't appear to be coming in, I brought soda.

It's diet, but that's the only thing we have without caffeine, and I didn't figure either of us needed that right now."

Adam took the can automatically.

"So. What brings you to my curb on a Wednesday night?"

"Why didn't Francesca tell you when things started moving from friendly to flirty?"

Asher opened the can and took a long drink. "You'd have to ask her for the definitive answer, but I'm guessing some—maybe a lot—is because she figured she could handle it and she didn't want to bother me with something that wasn't an issue. And, maybe, the flirting was nice. I'd been so caught up in work that I hadn't been making our relationship a priority. Not like I should have been. Why?"

Adam spun the can in his hands and finally popped the top and sipped before the whole story came spilling out.

"Huh." Asher set his can in a cup holder. "It's not really the same at all, is it?"

Adam shook his head. "Not really. But I don't know how to love someone who doesn't trust me."

"I think maybe you're making it bigger than it is."

Adam frowned.

"Hear me out. I'm not saying what she did was right, but when you add in what you said about her past and her reputation—and your initial reaction to both of those things? It...kind of makes sense. I don't think she doesn't trust you. I think she wanted to prove to you that she could handle it, that you could trust her."

"So...she proves I can trust her by lying to me?"

Asher sighed. "No, by diminishing the problem and trying to keep you from having to question her faithfulness."

Adam frowned at his soda. In a twisted, convoluted way that almost made sense. "Why didn't she just say that?"

"Did you give her the chance?"

"Four weeks." She'd had four weeks. Not that he'd been particularly approachable, but if it was important—if *he* was important—wouldn't she have made it happen?

"You're quiet."

"I'm thinking."

"The way I see it, you have two choices. You can keep thinking and see if time brings you back together, or you can go and make her talk to you. She's had four weeks, you said? Seems to me time isn't the answer anymore."

Adam swallowed. "Her friend said Sara was thinking of moving."

"Then time definitely doesn't seem like the right choice if you don't want to lose her forever."

Forever. A life without Sara. It made his insides shrivel into knots. "I don't."

"Tell her, man." Asher picked up his soda and pushed open the car door. "You wanna come in? You can sleep in the guest room."

"Nah, but thanks. I'll go home. I have some planning to do."

Asher punched Adam's arm. "That's the spirit. Make sure we meet her before the wedding."

Adam laughed. "If I can convince her to stay, I'll get Carol to grill."

Tomorrow. If he couldn't fix this, Sara was going to turn in her resignation tomorrow. The thought had plagued him through the morning. Finally, he'd rescheduled the contractor meetings he had for the afternoon and had driven to her office. He parked where he could see her car and waited, praying today was a day she'd head out for lunch.

Around one, she finally appeared. Her shoulders were hunched, her head down as she crossed the lot toward her car. Adam hopped out of the truck and angled toward her, reaching her door before she did.

Sara stopped, her eyebrows drawing together. "Adam."

"Hi."

"What are you doing here, Adam?"

Every time she said his name, it was a little beacon of hope shining into his shattered heart. "I needed to talk to you."

She crossed her arms, not a defensive posture, but more like she was giving herself a hug. "Why?"

Of course she wasn't going to make this easy. Adam sighed and stepped closer. She stepped back, bumping into the car. "Because I don't want to lose you. Not like this."

She laughed. "It's been a month. You're just now figuring that out?"

He took a deep breath and counted to ten, trying to keep the reins on the temper that wanted to erupt. Lashing out was only going to make it worse. "The phone works both ways, Sara."

"Okay. That's true." She turned her head and stared across the parking lot for several seconds before she looked at him. "So talk."

"Can I take you to lunch?"

"Yeah. Okay."

It wasn't a ringing endorsement, but he'd take it. At least she hadn't told him no. "Mind if I drive?"

She shrugged.

He turned and headed back to his truck, stopping on the passenger side to hold open the door for her. When she was seated, he closed it gently and rounded the hood. He'd gotten her in the truck. Now he just needed her to listen. And actually hear him.

The drive was quiet. Adam wasn't sure if he should start the conversation or wait until they were seated. The Afghan restaurant he had in mind wasn't fancy—the food was amazing, but the ambience was more fast food than anything. Still, casual was less intimidating, wasn't it?

"What's this place?"

"Um, Afghan. Their gyros are incredible. Or...there's a pizza place here, too, if you'd rather." Maybe this whole thing was a mistake.

"No, this is good. I haven't had a gyro in forever. Who knew this place was so close? Other than you, I guess."

He smiled.

She looked around when they entered. He tried to see it through her eyes. It definitely wasn't impressive. Did that count for or against him? He groaned. He needed to stop over thinking this whole thing. "So. A gyro?"

Sara nodded. "Sure. Thanks."

"Fries or a Greek salad?"

"How's the salad?"

"Good. Better than the fries."

She laughed. "Then why did you ask?"

"Choose a table. I'll be right there." A little distance was good. It would keep him from grabbing her hand and pulling her closer. He'd missed their conversations, and the hole in his heart when he thought their friendship was completely lost was immense. But he missed touching her, too. Was that wrong? He placed their order and waited as the men behind the counter filled it. Everything was made fresh, but it didn't take long. He carried the two takeout containers to the table where Sara sat. "Can we pray?"

"Okay."

Biting back a sigh at her continued one-word answers, he bowed his head, folding his hands on the table. Her fingers rested lightly on top of his and his heart leapt. "Dear Jesus, thank you for this food. Please bless it and the hands that prepared it. Lord, be with us in this conversation. Help us to know Your will for our relationship and to be able to hear and forgive one another. Amen."

"Amen." Sara moved her fingers away. "Our relationship? Do we still have one?"

"I'd like us to." There. It was out. He held her gaze, willing her to see his heart.

She looked away. "Why?"

So many different questions in just one word. It probably wasn't a good plan to ask her to clarify, so he went with his heart. "Because I love you. I'm still hurt. Maybe a little angry. Disappointed. But when it's all boiled down, I want you in my life. Loving you is a choice I want to keep making."

"It didn't seem like that when you said goodbye and walked out."

Adam stabbed at his salad with the plastic fork. "What would you have done if the situation was reversed?"

She was quiet as she took a bite of her own salad and chewed. "Probably the same thing. Look. I'm sorry. I was handling it."

"Were you ever going to tell me?"

Sara shook her head. "Not if I could avoid it."

"Why?"

She looked down at her food and poked at it. "It's humiliating."

That was unexpected. "How?"

"Luc...was probably the stupidest mistake of my life. And the way I found out about that stupidity destroyed my confidence. He just assumed I'd have no problem being his D.C. area girlfriend while he had a wife at home. Because I guess that's the kind of woman I'd become, at least in appearance."

"I don't think that of you."

"Not anymore. But you did before you knew me."

Adam nodded slowly. She wasn't wrong. "I listened to the gossip. I'm sorry."

"It doesn't matter. I won't let it. But when he showed up, it was like the whole of my past came roaring back to the present and tried to swallow me whole. I ignored him in Jamaica. He flirted, tried to get me to go to dinner with him, made it very clear that his wife was on board with an open relationship."

"Seriously? What a scum ball."

Her laugh was strained. "Yeah, well. He is that. I guess ignoring it wasn't enough. Or it started him worrying that I was going to ruin whatever scam he had going bilking churches out of money. I'm ashamed to say I had no plan at all to tell the pastor about him. I didn't want anyone knowing...even if it cost them money they couldn't afford."

Adam reached across the table and took her hand. She didn't pull away. Instead, her fingers curled around his.

"Next thing I know, I'm in the pastor's office and he's making accusations. So I called Ben and had him explain the truth of what happened last year with Luc's job. I wasn't sure he'd do it, at first. I wondered if they had some confidentiality agreement in place. If they do, Ben didn't seem to care. He explained it all and the pastor sent Luc packing. I think he probably warned the other pastors on the island, as well. I suspect word will spread and Luc's days of 'missionary work' are over."

"Good. You did the right thing."

Sara nodded. "But that's when the harassment started. And there was nothing anyone could do. I was going to get a new number and pray that it all went away. I wasn't trying to lie to you, I thought...there was no point in you being angry about it."

"It's my job to protect you, Sara. Or, at least, it was...and I'd like it to be again. Don't you trust me enough to share the bad things, too?"

"I didn't see it as a lack of trust. I...I'm sorry." A tear slipped down her cheek and she brushed it away. "I wasn't trying to hurt you."

"Can I ask you a question?"

She nodded, her expression guarded.

"Do you trust me?"

Sara closed her eyes and nodded.

"Will you forgive me for being angry and walking away? I promise not to do it again. I'll make you fight with me instead."

She laughed. "That's a deal. I love you. I tried not to."

Adam squeezed her hand. "I love you, too. Does that mean you'll stay?"

"You heard about that, did you?"

"Yeah. It jumpstarted my plans to bring you around by quite a bit."

"It turns out, I like it here. Maybe you really are the fresh start I've been waiting for."

26

Sara smiled at the text from Adam. It'd been two weeks since their lunch conversation and, after a few rocky moments, they were back on steady footing. The relationship seemed deeper, more solid, for having weathered the bump. It shouldn't have been this hard. It could've been so much worse. She'd actually gotten a job offer from the practice in Texas she'd applied to. Turning it down had been easy. She wasn't running—or hiding—from her problems anymore.

Adam had talked her into confronting Luc. They'd called him. Together. She grinned at the memory. Luc had tried to hedge, and then outright lie, but ultimately he'd backed off. Adam had seen to that. It was unlikely that he'd be bothering her again. They'd talked to Ben as well, and he was working on getting his company to be a little more open about Luc's behavior, at least within the sphere of the charities they coordinated with. There was no point letting Luc continue to fleece people. Not if they could stop it.

And tonight they were going out to celebrate the six-month anniversary of the day they'd met at Dunn River Falls in Jamaica. She'd lobbied to wait and celebrate their first date instead, but Adam had been determined. He'd said remembering that they could overcome obstacles in their relationship was just as important as celebrating the good times.

The knock at the door startled her. She pressed a hand to her jumping belly. They went out all the time. This was nothing new. Except it was an anniversary and that made it special. Sara opened the door and swallowed.

"Wow."

He grinned. "I think that's my line."

"Two years ago, I would've invited you in and we would've skipped dinner completely."

Adam took a deep breath, his eyes glinting. "Then let's get going before we're too tempted. There'll be time for that before long."

Her heart skipped a beat. They'd talked about marriage before and after the Luc ordeal, but it had always been abstract. Their plans, hopes, and dreams for what marriage looked like, nothing specific to the two of them being married. Maybe he was finally ready for that. Sara was.

She took his hand and pressed her lips to his. "Where are we going?"

"And ruin the surprise?" Adam shook his head. "You know me better than that."

She laughed. "I had to try."

They caught each other up on little pieces of their days as they drove. There wasn't much to say, they called and texted a lot during the day. She'd gotten in trouble twice at work for sneaking into the break room to check her texts. Not big trouble, but still. There was never going to be enough time spent with Adam. Not until they could go to sleep at night and wake up in the morning together. How long would that be?

They parked in a garage and stepped out onto the sidewalk near the shore of the Potomac in Old Town Alexandria.

"This is pretty. I've always liked Old Town. Are we eating down here?"

"Sort of." Adam took her hand and squeezed. "You don't get seasick, do you?"

Her eyebrows lifted. "Not to my knowledge."

"Excellent. Here we are."

She paused. The pier? A good-sized white ship was docked and a steady stream of couples and families were winding their way up the gangplank. Sara bounced on the balls of her feet and uttered a little squeal as she threw her arms around Adam. "A dinner cruise? I've always wanted to go on one of these!"

"You mentioned it once. I filed it away, seemed like the kind of thing that would work really well for a special date. Our six-month anniversary seemed like it qualified." Adam grinned.

Sara kissed him. "It really does. Thank you."

"My pleasure. Come on. We don't want to miss the boat."

Laughing, they crossed the street and got in the line to board the ship.

Adam had reserved a table for two by the window. They chatted and ate, looking out the window as they cruised up the river toward D.C. The sun was just setting as they finished dessert.

"Want to go out on the deck? We should be nearing the monuments before long." Adam scooted his chair back and held out his hand. "Or we can sit here. The table's ours for the whole cruise. There's dancing later, if you want, though I should warn you I haven't really danced since prom."

"That sounds about right. Dancing was never my forte. Who'd you go to prom with?" Sara took his hand and stood. "The deck sounds nice."

"Molly, actually."

"You went to prom with Molly?" Sara shook her head. "I didn't realize you'd known each other that long. Why aren't the two of you together?"

"We're better as friends. There's no chemistry. I tried, for a while, to create it. But..." He shrugged. "Anyway, now that she and Karl are engaged, it's pretty obvious the two of them belong together."

"Yeah. They're a good match, though I guess I'm surprised. It still seems fast?" Sara held her breath. His answer would tell her so much. She almost didn't want to hear it. What if...what if he agreed?

"I thought that at first. Even said something to that effect to Molly. But she reminded me that they weren't kids. They were grown, had been on their own and knew who they were and what they wanted. When she went through it, it all made sense." Adam shrugged. "They're doing pre-marital counseling with Pastor Brown.

From the things they've said, and listening to them do their homework together, it's pretty intense. They aren't going into anything blind."

Hope took root in Sara's heart. Maybe her plan wasn't as insane as it seemed. She hadn't been able to bring herself to breathe a word of her idea to Jen or Rebecca. They wouldn't understand. And while they'd been right, and she'd been wrong, about how to handle Luc, in this case...they couldn't know the right thing.

Sara walked to the rail and leaned on it, looking out as the lights twinkled on the river and they neared downtown.

Adam stepped behind her, wrapping his arms around her waist and leaning his cheek against hers. "Have I mentioned how much I love you?"

She warmed from her toes to the top of her head and shifted so her lips brushed against his. "I never mind hearing it. Adam...I love you. Marry me."

He blinked and then a slow smile spread across his face. Hands on her shoulders, he turned her so they were facing and reached into his pocket. "I wasn't sure I was going to use this tonight. But, since you asked so nicely."

Sara's eyes widened as he pulled a small velvet box from his pocket and flipped it open. She reached out and he snapped it shut.

"Where's mine?"

Sara drew her brows together. "What?"

"You asked me to marry you. Don't I get a ring?"

"But that...you have a ring for me."

"Sure. But I didn't ask you. You asked me. I think it's traditional for the asker to give the askee a ring." Adam's voice was tinged with laughter. "Isn't it?"

"I don't...Adam." He was teasing. She knew that. But her heart yearned for that ring to slide onto her finger. "Please?"

"Oh. You want this?"

Sara nodded.

"Then I guess we need to do this the right way." Adam sank to his knee, holding her hand and opening the ring box a second time. "Sara Reynolds, I love you. I can't think of anything better than spending the rest of my life choosing to love you, even when it's hard. Will you marry me?"

"Of course I will. I love you so much."

Grinning, Adam took the ring from its velvet bed and slid it on her finger.

Sara admired the glint of sparkle from the diamond on her finger for a moment before meeting and holding his gaze, her heart soaring. "Just remember, I asked you first."

Want a Free Book?

If you enjoyed A Tidbit of Trust and would like to read another of my books for free, you can get a free download simply by signing up for my newsletter here: http://bit.ly/2g0AGvf

Turn the page for a sneak peek at Chapter One of Wisdom to Know, the first book of the Grant Us Grace series that inspired the Taste of Romance books. Jackson Trent, the hero of the first Taste of Romance book, A Splash of Substance, appears as a house sitter in the Grant Us Grace books.

<u>Wisdom to Know</u>
Grant Us Grace, Book One

Chapter 1

"You look like a prostitute."

Lydia frowned. "Brad likes my legs."

Kevin admired the long, shapely legs of his best friend from where he was sprawled on her living room couch. "Won't you be cold if you show so much of them?"

"It's September, not the middle of January. It's still warm out." Aggravation written across her face, she patted her hem. "Besides, the skirt reaches the end of my fingertips."

"Your elbows are bent."

"That rule shouldn't apply to me, I have long fingers."

Kevin cocked a brow. "You wouldn't wear that to church."

"We're not going to church." Lydia shot him an impish grin. "Besides, there are a couple of guys there who wouldn't usually give me the time of day...maybe if I wore this, I'd get their attention."

"More than likely." Kevin shook his head. "Where are you going? You never did say."

"Dinner downtown, then to a club, in Georgetown I think."

"Bridge club?" He asked hopefully.

Lydia snickered. "Dance. But then you knew that. And before you ask, no, I don't know which club. But," she lifted a red-tipped finger to forestall his comment, "since it's Brad, it'll be either swing or salsa."

Kevin frowned. "Everyone is going to see your underwear in that skirt."

Lydia rolled her eyes.

Kevin started to speak several times before rubbing his forehead. "I'm just trying to look out for you, kiddo."

"Thanks, Mom."

"Didn't you just finish complaining that Brad treats you like an object?"

She gave a grudging nod.

"You think it might have something to do with clothing choices?"

Lydia crossed her arms. "I should be able to wear anything I want and still be treated with respect."

"Sure, in a perfect world. But seriously, Lyd, that outfit…" He paused and considered the short skirt too-snug top and shook his head. "It doesn't scream 'Respect me'."

Pouting, she pushed his feet out of the way and flopped onto the couch beside him. "I appreciate your concern."

Kevin snorted.

"No, I really do." She smiled and patted his knee. "You're like the brother I never had."

He winced.

"Still, a date with your almost fiancé is surely a reason to dress up, right? Or did you want me to wear something like that?" Lydia gestured to a conservative black jacket draped on the arm of the sofa.

"What's wrong with it?"

"That's for work. This is a date. You don't wear work clothes on a date."

Kevin stood, glancing at his watch, "Whatever, Lydia. I drove into McLean to see if you were free tonight, not to be a stand-in for a girlfriend. Or a brother. You look great and you know it." A brief, wistful look flashed across his features. "I'm sure Brad will agree." His hand on the knob of her apartment door, he turned and added with a resigned sigh, "You know where to find me when you get home and need to complain about how he spent the evening undressing you with his eyes."

"That's not fair, Kevin."

"Tell me about it," he muttered, slamming the apartment door behind him.

Author's Note

Thank you for reading A Tidbit of Trust! I hope that you enjoyed it! I would appreciate it if you'd help others enjoy it too by leaving a review! Word of mouth is how most people say they find new books to read, so I'd love it if you'd also consider telling your friends about it. Any success my books have is owed to readers like you who take the time to tell others about my stories. Thank you, from the bottom of my heart.

A Tidbit of Trust is the final book in the Taste of Romance series, and I feel like I owe my loyal readers an apology for how long it took to come out! This series took a little turn from what I intended, moving into themes that veered away from the foodie aspects I'd planned to incorporate all the way through, but I feel like the stories are better for having let them go where they did. I hope you agree. If you're new to the series and you'd like to catch up with all the couples you meet briefly inside, please consider going back to A Splash of Substance, book one in the series and starting from there. The series, in order, is A Splash of Substance, A Pinch of Promise, A Dash of Daring, A Handful of Hope, and finally A Tidbit of Trust.

If you enjoyed the Taste of Romance series, but haven't read anything else by me, I hope you'll take a look at the list of other books I've written in the front of this e-book (or on my website) and give something else a try.

You can always keep up to date with my writing news via my newsletter. There's a sign-up form at my website http://bit.ly/2g0AGvf and also on my author Facebook page http://www.Facebook.com/ElizabethMaddrey.

I continue to owe a huge debt of gratitude to my husband and sons for giving me the time to write, my sister for her unflinching support and encouragement, and my critique partners Valerie Comer, Lynellen Perry, Heather Gray and Jan Elder for catching all the times I use the same word six times in two paragraphs.

More than anything, I'm grateful that God continues to give me words and makes it possible for me to write them down.

I'd love to hear from you! You can connect with me on Facebook my webpage or via email.

About the Author

Elizabeth Maddrey began writing stories as soon as she could form the letters properly and has never looked back. Though her practical nature and love of computers, math, and organization steered her into computer science at Wheaton College, she always had one or more stories in progress to occupy her free time. This continued through a Master's program in Software Engineering, several years in the computer industry, teaching programming at the college level, and a Ph.D. in Computer Technology in Education. When she isn't writing, Elizabeth is a voracious consumer of books and has mastered the art of reading while undertaking just about any other activity.

Elizabeth is the author of more than ten books, both fiction and non-fiction. She lives in the suburbs of Washington, D.C. with her husband and their two incredibly active little boys.

www.ingramcontent.com/pod-product-compliance
Lightning Source LLC
Chambersburg PA
CBHW070700280626
47159CB00022B/1668

* 9 780997 883183 *